BUTTERFLY IN A JAR

Clean Mystery and Suspense

PATRICIA SNELLING

Published in New Zealand by Inthelight Publishing

A catalogue record for this book is available from the National Library of New Zealand

Martin Joyce – Cover Designer
Judith Little – Editing Support

****

Other Books by Author:

Last Ferry To Gulf Harbour (Ann Grieves Mysteries)
Murder In The Band Room (Ann Grieves Mysteries)
Missing On Lion Rock
When Hope Went South
Jessie's High Country Heart
Mack The Good Shepherd
Missing On Kawau
Unshakable (Peacehaven Series)
Broken Web (Peacehaven Series)
Rescue Net
Louis's Garden Party (Preschool book)

****

Website: patriciasnelling.com

****

Disclaimer

This novel is written in British English with New Zealand colloquialisms or Kiwi slang.

Chapter One

Meg Doyle leaned on the clothesline post, mesmerised by her latest garden treasure. This dazzling blue beauty was a rare find in a butterfly which had come from Australia—only occasionally visiting her garden.

She quietly placed the laundry basket on the footpath, wishing she had her digital camera in her pocket, which always captured spectacular close-ups.

While gazing at the awesome creature that possessed an unusually large wingspan, a swishing sound nearby startled her, and in an instant, the fragile blue creature lay stunned inside the butterfly net.

Meg swung around as her husband Lyle stood with a triumphant smirk on his face.

'Why did you do that? You know it's one of my special ones. I'd got so close to it and could see every tiny detail. You've got enough in your collection.' Meg's voice broke up. She was a quivering mess, both from anguish and inner rage at this monster of a man. *Sadist*, she called him under her breath.

'Ah—don't be such a wimp, woman! You know I don't have this one in my collection. You're far too sentimental for your own good— you need to toughen up!'

Meg clenched her teeth tight. She wanted to give him a barrage of her anger straight back, but her throat seized up—speechless with wrath as she continued to take the washing off the line.

Lyle grunted and stomped inside the house, carrying his booty in the net with Meg in tow. He walked straight into the kitchen and leaned over to reach for the large preserving jar on the window ledge.

Meg froze in horror. She set down the laundry basket and thrust out a hand to stop him, but he pushed her back with an abrupt swipe of his arm.

'Get back!' Lyle bellowed, laying the net on the bench and unscrewing the lid from the jar. He eased the butterfly from the net with cupped hands, sliding it into the glass prison.

Meg's inner rage deepened at her powerlessness and in trepidation of what she knew would come next. People wouldn't believe her if she told them her husband sadistically watched these beautiful creatures flail around in the jar, slowly suffocating to death. Of course, she knew he did it to hurt her, too. It seemed to enthral him to see his wife squirm, and the longer the better.

The porridge Meg ate at breakfast had moved from her gut to her throat, doing somersaults behind her tongue, and once again, she walked off into the bathroom and locked the door, weeping her heart out.

'Meg—get back here!'

The voice from the kitchen made her skin crawl. Living in the same house with this man's maniacal tirades was becoming more than she could bear.

Wetting a flannel and wiping her eyes, she peered in the mirror and saw that deep lines added years to her appearance.

She trudged back to the kitchen, trying not to glance at the frantic blue beauty that flitted from one side of the jar to the other and turned her head away.

'We're going fishing, so get the gear ready— it's on the back doorstep,' Lyle roared. 'I'm shooting up to the grocery store, and when I get back, I want to head off to the beach.'

'Fishing now? It's late in the day and getting cold. The wind is up.'

'I don't care,' he snapped—his face twisting with contempt. 'You know we have the Farmer's Market in the morning, and I promised a customer some fish.'

Oh, blast—I completely forgot it was Saturday tomorrow. His darned obsession with fishing!

Meg let out a long sigh and massaged her temples. She was at her wit's end. There was no escape, as Lyle rarely let her out of his sight, and his obsessive-compulsive control prevented her from having any autonomy in her life.

He had been an inventor of all kinds of strange money-making ventures in his time and had designed and built a drone prototype.

These days, he and Meg lived off the money he earned from royalties paid by a manufacturer who had purchased his prototype from him. He also produced a small income from wood-turning projects he created in his workshop on a lathe. Sometimes he used drones to deliver little packages around the piece of coast near their home—a popular item being a kauri wooden salt and pepper mill set.

Lyle was a keen angler, and the fish he caught were in demand at the local Farmer's Market in Langhome as well as his wooden crafts. Meg couldn't understand why he bothered doing all of this when they didn't actually need the money.

Lyle often used drones to stalk her, and now her tolerance had worn thin. Something deep inside was unleashing itself, ready to break out.

***

Meg walked to the lounge window and glanced towards the driveway. Lyle had not yet returned. Hurrying back to the kitchen, she unscrewed the preserving jar, opened the window and let the butterfly go outside. For an instant it hovered as if to say thank you and then soared high and fluttered away. She picked up the jar and dropped it hard on the floor, just as a car skidded up their gravel driveway and screeched to a halt.

Oh no, he's back already!

Before Meg could think of what she would say, the front door swung open.

'What the heck are you doing, woman? Ah, I see what you've done!'

Lyle lurched forward, grabbing the back of her neck, pushing her to the ground on her knees.

'You can clean this up—I know what you're playing at. Think you've outsmarted me, do you? We'll see about that! Pick up every bit of glass!'

5

Meg was too incensed to cry. She had done plenty of weeping since the first week they had married. That was when all the abuse began. But now she could take no more. This last episode was the straw to break the camel's back.

'I'll get the dustpan before I cut my fingers.'

'No, you won't.' Lyle pushed her down as she tried to stand then reached for a nearby newspaper and thrust it at her. 'You should have thought about that before you deliberately smashed the jar.'

Stand over tactics—she was used to that. But now she'd become desperate. The sight of blood trickling down her legs was sufficient for him to retreat as she moved towards the rubbish bin with the glass wrapped in newspaper. Her agitation caused her to pare the skin of her index finger with a thin shard of glass, but she denied the pain. After disposing of the glass, still seething, she hurried into their bedroom to dress for a chilly late-afternoon outing—fishing off the rocks near home.

This was the beginning of the end. Her menace of a husband had gone too far. There had to be a way of escape—somehow, someway, she would find it.

Chapter Two

Meg wished she possessed a much warmer jacket, as the southwesterly wind pierced her soul. Her back and joints ached again from the tension and stress of her altercation with Lyle, who strode way ahead carrying only two fishing rods over his shoulder.

The heavy bucket containing his fish bait, tackle box, cutting board and two drink bottles slowed Meg down. No wonder she was hobbling.

Lyle's fishing spot was not one shared by most of the locals, who usually threw their lines off the end of the long pier or from the flat, rocky ledge nearby. Instead, he took the risk of casting his rod off the rocks at the end of Burns Point. Everyone knew it was a dangerous West Coast beach location where several fishers had drowned in the past. Perhaps Lyle had a death wish, Meg had always thought.

The one kilometre walk to the fishing spot carrying the bucket gave her blisters in the palm of her hand.

By the time she arrived at the Point, Lyle was already fuming, waiting for his gear so he could cast his line.

'Confounded woman! Are you deliberately trying to hold me up? Where's that bait—give it here!'

Meg felt like throwing the bucket at him. She asked herself why she had put up with his bullying for so long. Her sister, Angela, had repeatedly insisted that she leave him. But where could she go with no money of her own while everything they possessed was in his name—their bank accounts, the Peugeot car, home and furniture?

The shrill screech of seagulls fighting over dried fish remnants on a rock startled Meg back to reality. She lifted out the small, scarred cutting board from the bucket and placed it on a flat edge of a rock they usually used to chop bait, as well as the whole fish which Lyle had removed from the freezer before they left.

She picked up the razor-sharp fishing knife and cut a small piece of bait and handed it to the figure looming over her.

'Hurry up, woman. It'll be dark before I throw my first line out. Get going with the rest of it!'

Meg's fingers numbed as the brisk onshore wind whistled passed her ears. This was a ritual when fishing with Lyle. He lorded it over her, standing on an elevated rock like King Kong, she thought, when in fact, he was just a coward, enjoying himself pushing a woman around.

Her rear end was sore from sitting on the hard surface, and although she could change position, it would be no more comfortable. What she needed was a small cushion or even a folded towel to sit on, but that would mean extra weight to carry in the bucket. The sticking plaster on her index finger fell off, and she sucked her wound to soothe it.

Lyle muttered something, and when she looked up, he was grappling with a large King Fish that took some effort from reeling in. When he finally brought it to shore, he took great delight in releasing the hook from its mouth right in front of her. Meg cringed.

He extracted a fish brain spike from his tackle box. 'It's about time you learnt how to gut a fish instead of leaving me to do it all!'

Meg shuddered as he relished making her watch him pierce the creature's brain before slitting its throat, letting it bleed out into the

9

water below. He sliced its belly to let the innards ooze out and threw them to a hungry seagull.

'Here—this one will be worth a few dollars, I'd say. Stick it in the sack. You can clean the next one.'

Meg always felt the urge to answer back when he snarled at her in a derogatory manner but knew to restrain it, as he would only give her a back-hander. The last time he did that, she lost a tooth requiring expensive dental work. Lyle had reluctantly paid for this but made her suffer in other ways.

She removed the jute sack from the bucket and placed the fish inside.

'Can we go back now? I'm getting cold and sore from sitting on the rocks.' Meg asked through gritted teeth.

'What? Of course not! I need a couple more like that one. I told you I received a few orders last week at the market.'

Meg shivered. 'Well, that wind is biting, and it's freezing sitting here. I could walk back to get the car and then find something comfortable to sit on.'

Lyle scoffed. 'We're not wasting money on petrol when we only live a stone's throw from here. You'll just have to wait—that's all.'

Meg felt her blood pressure suddenly shoot up and drew in a deep breath to stop her head from spinning. She watched Lyle prepare his line for the next cast, while envisaging a way of escape from this madness.

'Bring the bait, will you?' he snarled.

Meg hauled herself up and gathered the pieces of fish, wondering why he couldn't walk over and get the bait, but kept her thoughts to herself—for now.

'What's that? You've cut it too small! What do you expect me to catch with that—sprats? You'll have to chop up some more.'

Despite his remonstrations, he picked up a few pieces of the bait and attached them to the hooks while Meg looked on.

'Well, don't stand there gawping—get to it!'

He cast his line and stood with his back to Meg, puffed up and enjoying his narcissism while Meg almost choked on her contempt that struggled for freedom of speech as it stifled her breath.

As she turned around to fetch more bait, a huge rogue wave scooped Lyle up and rocketed him off the ledge and into the waves. While Meg stood staring in disbelief, he flailed about in the cold sea, trying to grasp hold of a rock, but the waves were too rough.

'Don't leave me here—you know I can't swim,' he shrieked, spluttering, while taking in gulps of sea water.

His bony white fingers frantically waved about above the water, grappling to clutch a rock as wave after wave thwarted his efforts.

In desperation, he continued to haul himself over the ledge and slid back down again, defeated as his heavy leather boots weighed him down. Now he'd lost control for the first time in his life.

'Pick up my spare rod next to you and give me one end,' he bellowed.

Meg glanced down at the rod, but her body wouldn't move, glued to the spot as she watched without a sympathetic bone in her body. For her, this was life or death, as she felt she'd come to the end of the road. Since their wedding day, he had systematically drained every ounce of pity from her, and the supply was now empty.

Something inside her snapped, and for the first time since her marriage to Lyle, she found her voice. An empowering revelation suddenly dawned on her—finally grasping that she was the butterfly in the jar and had been since that fateful day she had agreed to be his wife. But she was about to be set free.

'Now you know how it feels to flail around trying to save yourself—gasping for breath—just like my butterflies,' she fumed. 'You showed them no mercy, and this is what it felt like for them.'

Meg's heart had grown cold after years of brow-beating and daily subjugation. It was her life or his, and today, for the first time in her married life, she chose to live. Leaving all the fishing gear on the rocks, she walked home in the shadows of sundown as teardrops ran down her frozen cheeks. It would soon be dark, and the beach was empty.

Chapter Three

When Meg arrived through the door of her lounge, she crumpled in a heap on the sofa with her head in her hands, thinking what just occurred had been a bad dream and it would all go away. But flashbacks of Lyle's fingers scraping down the rock and the gurgling sound in the water as she turned and walked away haunted her.

She glanced at the clock on the wall. It was 7 pm and darkness had set in. Perhaps she'd better go back and check if Lyle is actually dead.

Grabbing the car keys and locking the door behind her, Meg reiterated in her mind what she would do if he had drowned. Speeding along the road, she barely missed a cat which shot out in front of the vehicle, further adding to her trauma.

Stopping the car in front of the track, she was perturbed at the thought of stepping out into the dark, alone. It was an isolated area and at night Meg felt it was awfully creepy and not a safe place for a woman to wander around by herself.

She put her cell phone in her pocket, ready in case of an emergency. Using the powerful torch she'd grabbed before leaving the house, Meg made her way to the rocks, nervously looking behind her while stepping over pieces of driftwood and seaweed.

At last, arriving at the fishing spot, Meg clambered up onto the place where the cutting board with bait, sharp knife and Lyle's spare rod lay on the rock exactly where she'd left them.

Shining the torch into the sea where he'd fallen, there was no sign of him—only ripples made by small fish swimming around the rocks. Although the tide was on the turn, the water level was still high, and rough waves continued to crash over the rocks. *He must have been washed out to sea*, she thought, her heart pounding with angst.

She wanted to curl up in a ball and pretend it wasn't happening. But thinking quickly on her feet, she realised she had to make it look as though Lyle hadn't drowned but had returned home from fishing.

After throwing the pieces of smelly fish bait into the sea, Meg put all the tackle back into the bucket, as well as the sack with the large fish as proof that her husband had a successful catch that day. In her mind she had already concocted quite a story to tell Lyle's elderly mother who lived in England if she started interrogating her, although he'd not seen her in years and his father had already died.

Meg was sure her sister Angela would understand and celebrate his disappearance.

The eeriness of dusk and the remoteness of the area made her shudder. Meg picked up Lyle's spare rod, and as she was about to step off the rocky ledge back onto the sand with the bucket, something shiny caught her eye.

When she flashed the torch amongst the rocks, his other rod appeared with its line tangled around a jagged outcrop. 'Thank God!'

Placing everything back on the ground, she cautiously edged her way over to the point of the protruding rod and pulled. It wouldn't budge. Taking out the fishing knife from the bucket, she sliced the catgut that trapped the line. Once it was free, she unravelled the rest of it and wound it around the rod. It was still a tangled mess.

It wasn't easy carrying two rods with the heavy bucket and the torch while making her way back to her car, but she didn't want to draw attention to the fact that she was with Lyle when he had drowned. People might ask why she hadn't alerted the coastguard or the police.

Her story was straightforward, she thought. *While accompanying Lyle fishing at dusk, I became chilled by a sudden cold onshore wind and returned home while Lyle continued fishing.*

If anyone had seen her walking home alone, her explanation would be that Lyle stayed behind at Burns Point.

The minute that Meg arrived inside the house, she put the King fish straight into the freezer and washed the fishy smell off her hands.

Exhausted—all she could eat was a banana washed down with a glass of milk, and then pulled back the duvet and crashed into bed, oblivious of that day's tumultuous shenanigans.

***

Meg woke the next morning with her head pounding, and when she swallowed, it felt like a thousand razor blades were cutting into her throat.

The space next to her in the bed was empty. Had Lyle got up already?

Meg recalled the terrible nightmare she'd experienced during the night when she'd pushed Lyle off a rock into the sea. She shuddered as she remembered walking away and leaving him floundering and taking in water.

Meg would never do that—leave someone to drown. But now she was confused. Hurrying onto the back porch, she couldn't believe her eyes. There was Lyle's bucket of tackle with the torch lying in it. His tangled fishing rod stood leaning against the wall with the other one next to it.

Surely not. That was in my bad dream too.

Her head still pounded as she washed back the painkillers with a glass of water and remembered she'd not eaten a proper meal except for a banana the day before. They were supposed to have had fresh fish for dinner the previous evening, but that didn't happen.

Meg forced down a small serving of yogurt and a handful of blueberries to keep her strength up. It was about the only food she could swallow easily.

She was in a muddle, having trouble separating her dreams from reality and tried hard to remember what happened the night before. In the past, she'd suffered from amnesia, or memory lapses, especially after receiving a beating from Lyle, or when he'd pushed her over. Today was one of those days.

Meg's phone vibrating in her pocket interrupted her mental meanderings. She hesitated, checking the Caller ID first—afraid it was Lyle, but when she saw it was her sister, she answered.

'Angela! You're up early on a Saturday. How are you?'

'To be honest, I'm more interested in how you are. Can you talk? I haven't heard from you in weeks, and the last time Lyle had given you a swollen nose. What's going on now?'

'I'm not sure—he went off somewhere last night or early this morning and didn't let me know where he was going. Yesterday he mentioned he might go out late on Friday night with a friend.'

'What friend—where would he go at night without you?'

'Well—he used to go up to the casino sometimes with his friend, Chuck—perhaps he went there and crashed at his house afterwards. He was in a right mood after I let a prize butterfly go free.'

'Swine! I tell you, Meg—that bloke is evil. You've got to toughen up and leave him. I remember you said once when you went with them to the casino, you caught them both leering at young teenagers. He's up to no good again.'

'I know, Angela. But I've got nowhere to go. Everything we own is in his name, except my mobile phone, thanks to you and Pete.'

Meg was grateful she had the support of Angela and her husband. When Lyle had smashed her previous pre-pay phone she'd purchased with the proceeds from her art sales, they stepped in and confronted him. They were forthright—insisting Meg should always possess a mobile phone for emergencies—especially with her head injury, which he'd caused, and subsequent amnesia.

But now, the discomfort Meg felt deceiving her sister made her shudder. Stomach acid surged into her throat.

'You can move in with us. Pete won't mind— he always said you should get away from him and stay with us, at least until you find your own way.'

'Did he? That's kind of him.'

'Well, you know he never took a shine to Lyle for the bully he is. Look—if he doesn't come home tonight, pack up your things and come here, and then we can see what to do after that.'

'Thanks, Sis. I might just do that.'

'Make sure, if you do come, to bring all your personal papers and whatever documents you can dig up regarding your home ownership, insurances and so forth. What about the bank statement showing your share of the inheritance we received when Mum and Dad died in the accident—where did you deposit the money?'

'Into my savings account. But shortly after we married, Lyle persuaded me to transfer the funds into one of his personal accounts, which he said he would use to purchase our first home. All I have left is the money I've made from my butterfly paintings. Lyle took control of all the finances, and our accounts are in his name only.'

'Don't worry—the bank can trace that original payment. It was cunning of him to put the house in his name, especially as the money from your inheritance paid for it. We're going to find out what he is up to—believe me, I won't let him hurt you anymore.'

'I'm hope he can't record our conversations. He always knows when you and I have been talking when he sees the phone bill.'

'What happened to the pre-pay cell phone I helped you purchase with money from your painting sales? I've tried ringing it repeatedly and it sounds out of service.'

'Lyle discovered it in my jacket pocket. I told him I only kept it for emergencies, but he went ahead and confiscated it.'

'I'll get you a new one on that account we set up for you before—once you arrive at our house. We'll sort you out, Meg—you just can't go on living like this. Just get yourself around here as soon as you can.'

Chapter Four

After finishing her phone conversation with Angela, Meg spent the rest of the day searching out the papers and documents relating to the house and bank accounts. She printed off copies of everything she might need to show how Lyle had taken her funds, and then replaced each one back into the filing cabinet, all the while scared stiff that he might walk in and catch her in the act of looking at them.

Even though in her sane mind, Meg knew Lyle was probably dead, she kept getting strange flashbacks of him floundering in the water calling out for help but could not decide if it actually happened, or whether he had been acting out the scene to keep her subservient to his demands. *If that were the case, he could turn up at any time*, she thought.

After a brutal beating from Lyle some years ago when he had completely lost his temper,

Meg's clinicians had diagnosed her with Transient Global Amnesia—a condition that occasionally caused her to have severe memory lapses.

The doctors explained that it could be brought on by heavy stress. To make matters worse, when she was under a great deal of emotional tension—which was often—she suffered frightening nightmares.

Meg looked at the tangled line on the rod, wondering how it had got into that state. She tried hard to remember if Lyle had gone fishing the previous day. He always looked after his gear well and would never leave it in that condition, so he must have rushed off to an emergency.

She would have to prepare herself in case he indeed had left her. But surely, he would have taken all his personal documents and papers. His passport was still there, so he hadn't planned on moving far away.

I'll phone Chuck. Perhaps Lyle is with him if they went to the casino last night.

After a brief conversation with his friend, Meg caved in on the sofa and lay back, exhausted.

What's going on? She wondered. Chuck denied having seen Lyle and said he would ask some of his mates if they'd laid eyes on him on

Friday night, but Meg urged him not to do so in case there was a perfectly simple explanation for his absence. She knew from experience that if he found out she'd been troubling his friends, there would be hell to pay.

Dog-tired after sorting through Lyle's documents and the trauma of the previous night, Meg lay on her bed for a quick nap—still desperately trying to get her head around what was going on.

There was someone yelling in her room, frightening her awake. She found the screeching sound had come from her own throat. It was that nightmare again, and it felt so real. She kept seeing herself pushing Lyle into the sea. *Is that what happened for real?*

A chill in the air snapped her back to the present when she realised she'd forgotten to close the bedroom window. Glancing at her wristwatch, the brief nap Meg had intended turned out to be a long sleep–it was 6 pm. But these unwanted thoughts and bad dreams were weighing her down. Perhaps she'd just been under far too much stress. And any minute, Lyle could walk through the front door.

Meg looked in the freezer for leftovers, and to her surprise, there was a whole gutted King fish lying on the top shelf, and it puzzled her how it got there—its frozen gaze resembling that of Lyle when he was in one of his rages aimed at her.

She forced herself to eat a couple of boiled eggs mashed onto a slice of bread, made more palatable with avocado. The smooth, bland textures of the food items were all she could manage as they slid down her throat easily. She knew she had to keep her strength up now, as the time had come for her to take care of herself.

The phone vibrated in her pocket and spooked the living daylights out of her.

'Angela—sorry, I've just woken up. I was exhausted.'

'Well, what's the verdict—has he come home?'

Meg hesitated, confused—not knowing how to answer. 'No, I haven't seen him yet. But there is something that's been troubling me—bad dreams. Oh, no matter. It's just my mind playing tricks on me again.'

'What are you trying to say, Meg—what's happened? I've known you all my life and you can't hide anything from me.'

'I forgot to tell you that our car is still in the driveway in front of the garage. Lyle must have got a ride with a friend, but I've heard nothing from him.'

'What were you going to tell me about those bad dreams you're having?'

'Nothing—I can't remember now. As I said, it's probably me being stressed out. I'm not myself right now.'

'I want you to pack up and come here—at least until we know what's happened to Lyle. Pete and I will help you find him.'

Meg hesitated. 'But what if he doesn't want to be found? He might just want to be rid of me—he kept saying it often enough.'

'Well, that's what we'll have to work out.'

'I'll come over soon. I have a few things to sort out here first. Perhaps in a day or two, if that's alright. I need to get my affairs in order before I leave the house.'

'Make sure you do. I can't leave you in this situation, not knowing whether something more sinister has happened to him. You might be in danger yourself.'

'I'd suspected he'd gone away on a fishing spree with one of his friends, but all his rods and tackle are still here.'

'That's a shame—otherwise I would guess he may have fallen in the tide while he was fishing.'

Meg almost dropped her phone with that bombshell. Something terrible resonated within her, but she couldn't understand what.

Chapter Five

Private Investigator Ann Grieves decided to take a break from her ritualistic walk with her Beagle dog, Scout, along the boulevard. Although Ann loved everything about Cockle Cove, occasionally she preferred beaches where Scout could have a long run off his lead.

After bundling him into the back of her Land Rover, she drove along the coast to Cornwall Bay—her favourite seaside.

The lengthy foreshore covered in golden sand was an ideal place for Scout, where he thoroughly enjoyed chasing seagulls or jumping over the white foam in the shallow waves. Ann would normally keep him on a lead, but at this beach, dogs were permitted to be unleashed to exercise on the beach.

There was no one else there except a lone figure sitting on an upturned dinghy. And as

Ann drew closer, she saw the outline of a woman sitting with her head in her hands. Ann approached with a welcoming smile and then recognised the woman's face.

'I think we've met before. Angela—isn't it? Didn't you used to sing in the choir with your sister at St Andrews? I remember you helped us out at my husband Terry's funeral, and then you suddenly disappeared.'

'Yes—we shifted further away, and it made sense to attend a church closer to home.'

'I get up there when I'm not busy on a case, and Reverend Thomas is still Vicar.'

'Oh, yes—I remember when you both used to play brass instruments in the church. What do you mean, you're on a case?'

'I'm a private detective handling all kinds of criminal investigations—from domestics to severe felonies. Although I prefer to stick to the less challenging ones.'

Angela's face changed. When Ann had first greeted her, she was just a little tense. Now her eyes spoke of intense sadness as she pulled out a tissue and blew her nose.'

'Is everything alright—have I said something to upset you?'

Angela's face turned red, as did the colour of her neck, in contrast to her white skin.

'No, it's nothing like that. I've just had some upsetting news about my sister, and I don't know what to do.'

'Maybe I can help. I recall you had a younger sibling called Meg, and even way back then you had your concerns.'

'That's right—when she married that brute of a man, Lyle, who's not fit to be called a husband.'

Ann looked around for Scout, who was busy playing with something on the beach.

'Sorry—just a moment. I'd better check my dog isn't eating a dead fish. I'll be back in a tick.'

Ann hurried off, aware she'd interrupted Angela, who was about to offload a burden. After sorting out the dog, she hastened back to her side and joined her on the seat.

The distraught woman came right out with it. 'He's missing, Meg told me. It looks like he left her completely with no warning.'

Ann grimaced. 'Oh! Did he give her no warning at all?'

'Nothing—but Meg told me that the abuse has escalated recently.'

Ann nodded, having already guessed that this might be the case after the murmurings she'd heard in the church when Meg was still a parishioner there.

'Is she managing? I expect it has traumatised her considerably.'

'That's just it—I don't know what's going on. You see—my sister suffers from a medical condition which causes her to have blackouts and lose her memory. It's called amnesia and it can happen spontaneously, often when she's under a great deal of stress.'

Ann hesitated, as though in deep thought. 'I'm familiar with such a disorder—I think it's called Transient Global Amnesia.'

'Oh—you've heard of it?'

'Yes—I've handled a few criminal cases where the perpetrator of a crime had a complete memory block and couldn't remember committing a serious felony.'

'Well, that's not in my sister's case. He's the felon, not her. She has suspected that he has been involved with another woman for some time now. He often leaves home for a few days at a time on so-called business trips,' Angela stammered.

'Where does he go?'

'Everywhere—he is contracted to a large multinational manufacturing company called *Air Tech,* who bought his drone prototype when he sold his factories. They continue to produce them in Australia and New Zealand, and Lyle receives the royalties. He travels around the country offering technical support and training to users and often goes overseas.'

'Mmm—that sounds ever so convenient for him. How did he meet Meg?'

'At one of his entrepreneurial seminars he once conducted in Auckland. She wanted to start her own small business as a graphic designer.'

'Wow, that sounds innovative—good for her!'

Angela's face changed as the corners of her mouth drew downwards. 'It was—but Lyle wrecked her chances of starting anything and she never fulfilled her dream. Once she married him, he stopped her from running her own business or getting a proper job. He ruined her life.'

'Look—tell Meg I'm a retired Detective Inspector working as a qualified private investigator and have a great deal of experience tracking missing relatives. I can help her for a reasonable fee, and if money is a problem, she may qualify for legal aid.'

'Is that right? I'll talk to her about it. Payment will not be difficult once she can access their money, but all their bank accounts are in Lyle's name.'

'Tell her not to worry about that right now. It may have to go to court, and then an attorney will help her sort it.'

'Well, I'll need to get her consent before I bring anyone else in on her domestic situation. She doesn't want to report him as missing to the police, as he may have just taken off for a few days to frighten her into submission.'

Ann observed the deep furrows of anguish on Angela's brow. 'Right you are.' She dived into her jacket pocket. 'Here—take my card and phone me any time. I've just finished working on a substantial criminal case and am free right now. Tracking an unfaithful spouse would be a breath of fresh air for me after that last fiasco.'

'Thanks, Ann. I'll be in touch if she's interested in getting help.'

Chapter Six

Meg was convinced after scanning the beach for the last three days for Lyle's body that it had been washed far out to sea. Burns Point, where Lyle had been fishing on that fateful day, was part of the Manukau Heads, which was a dangerous stretch of sea that was deep and turbulent. Many fishermen in boats had drowned trying to cross the bar to the land on the other side, and on each occasion the Search and Rescue teams, known to the locals as SAR, had given up looking for them. Although Lyle had lost friends in those waters, he continued to fish off the Point without a life jacket.

Meg had been plagued by unwanted thoughts and memories of Lyle falling into the sea. She had now convinced herself that it quite possibly could have happened with her looking on. She also recalled how angry she was when he captured her special butterfly and left it to die, and the hatred that had built up inside her. But she'd decided to carry on the charade of pretending that Lyle had abandoned her and would have to work fast to cover her tracks once deciding to go through with it.

Remembering the invitation Angela had given her to stay with them for a while, Meg knew that she must first get rid of Lyle's personal effects from the house, as if he had left her and taken them with him.

She had woken early before sunrise and made a coffee to wake herself. After removing Lyle's documents from his office, she used his printer to make copies of important files to keep for herself and kept them aside.

After tying the originals with string into a bundle, she attached a small brick to it and placed the package into a calico bag.

Before tying up the handles of the bag, Meg thought carefully about what a deserting spouse would do with their personal items. In the bag she included Lyle's passport and what original business files she could find, knowing that most of them would be stored on his computer.

She bolted down a bowl of yogurt with muesli. Then in the dark, she carried the bag out to the car—relieved that the neighbours couldn't see her over their tall hedge.

When Meg arrived at the lookout on top of the hill overlooking the blowhole, the sun had begun to show its face above the horizon. She hurried—looking all around—making sure there was nobody in sight.

Walking cautiously down to the viewing platform that protruded over the powerful turbulent waters below, a southerly wind nipped at her neck. Placing the calico bag with Lyle's documents on the ground, she zipped up her jacket.

White foam billowed underneath Meg as she aimed for the middle of the cauldron of chaotic water and not the rocks. After heaving the bag over the side of the metal barrier, she watched as it disappeared and waited. Soon the water would settle down for a few minutes before the turbulence wound up again. Finally, the water was smooth, and as she fixed her gaze on the spot where she had thrown the bag—it was calm, and there was no evidence of anything she'd tossed below.

'Thank goodness, it's gone,' she murmured. 'No one will ever find it down there.' *The papers will disintegrate in minutes with the velocity of those waves*, she convinced herself.

For a moment she froze—thinking her keys were in the bag she'd just thrown in the tide until her hand found them safely inside her jacket pocket. That gave her a shake-up. She couldn't get out of there quick enough and drove home ready to move onto her next covert plan.

***

Meg arrived home feeling triumphant—so much more confident and self-empowered than a few days earlier, knowing that she was gradually removing Lyle from her life—and with each step, she reinforced her mental alibis. It had to appear as though he had suddenly abandoned her. If he had done that, she knew he would have taken most of his belongings along with him. The personal documents were the first things that came to her mind. Now she planned to hide more of his belongings.

Meg tried to devise a plan. First, there was his fishing tackle box and rods, which she could either bury in the garden or take to a charity shop. But the second option would be risky, as someone could recognise her. No—the best plan would be to dig a deep hole in the private native forest behind the house and hide his stuff there.

Meg checked the phone and saw there was a missed call from Angela. It must have been while she was by the blowhole. Meg knew Angela was waiting for her to move out and stay with her and Pete, but she'd pushed it out of her mind for now, feeling the responsibility of keeping herself off the hook—from being implicated in her dreaded husband's death.

Now to sort the fishing gear. She went out to the garden shed and pulled on a pair of gumboots before lifting a shovel off its hook. The fishing tackle, which she'd packed into a cardboard box, along with both of Lyle's dismantled rods, lay where she'd left them the night before on the back doorstep.

Meg carried the items up through the back of the terraced garden leading into a small forest that bordered her backyard. There was no access for the public—the perfect hiding place—or at least, she hoped.

It was dark in the bush, apart from a few small gaps in the trees filtering sunlight. She chose the shadiest part of the forest to dig the hole.

To her relief, the friable, sweet-smelling earth was soft. It was going to be an easy feat.

After pulling on a pair of old gardening gloves, Meg started digging. When the hole was deep enough, she placed the dismantled fishing rods inside with the box of tackle and then stopped and went back to the house.

'I may as well bury the rest of Lyle's things in that hole together with the fishing gear,' she muttered, throwing the soiled gloves in the kitchen rubbish bag.

She pulled out a pair of rubber safety gloves Lyle kept in good supply when handling fish for the market. After gathering up the cell phone and laptop Lyle had left lying on the dining table when he'd gone fishing, Meg placed the items in a plastic bag and buried them in the forest with the fishing paraphernalia.

She dragged a decayed log across the burial site and scattered twigs and leaves over the area. After discarding the gloves in the household waste, she placed the plastic sack at the front gate for the collection later that day—congratulating herself on how well she had managed the coverup. *No one would ever know.*

Chapter Seven

While Meg was hurrying to pack up the car with her belongings to take to Angela's house, a white Ford Ranger Ute pulled up in the driveway. She cringed, seeing that he was one of Lyle's fishing mates.

'Meg! You look as though you're off on holiday—Lyle didn't say he was going away. Heading anywhere interesting?'

'Sorry—he's not here.'

Meg had only met this man once and wasn't sure what to tell him.

'Any idea when he'll be back? I wanted to take him fishing with me tonight if he's free.'

Meg swallowed hard, as if a marble was stuck in her throat. 'I ... don't know. He went away without telling me, and I haven't seen him for a few days.'

She thought it was the best thing to say without letting on he was missing.

'That wasn't decent of him. I thought he would be a bit more considerate.' The man grimaced and gave her a sympathetic look.

'We had … a kind of argument and he stalked off in a huff.'

'Yeah—I know he can fly off the handle a bit. If you see him, say that Larry called. His phone must be off—I've tried it several times.'

'Yes, I can't get hold of him either—but I'll let him know you were looking for him.'

Larry smiled, waved and drove off without any notion that Lyle had disappeared off the face of the earth.

Satisfied she'd carried her story off well, Meg was desperate to have a needed break from all the drama. She continued to pack the rest of the car, eager to get away from the house and warned her sister she was on the way.

***

On her arrival, Angela and Pete gave her a sympathetic reception.

'Here, Meg. Let me help carry your belongings up to the house,' said Pete, who had met her in the driveway.

41

'You can have Beth's room while she is away at Otago University,' said Angela, who led her up the hallway.

'Are you sure? I wouldn't want to take over.'

Meg looked at the framed drawings hanging on the wall in their daughter's room. 'Did she do these? They're good.'

'Yes—she was studying fine arts but has changed course and is doing law now.'

'Clever girl. Excuse me while I go back to the car and bring the rest of my luggage inside.'

Angela followed her into the lounge. 'I'll put on the kettle—I've made pikelets.'

Meg finished unloading the car and left everything in her new room while she joined Meg and Pete for afternoon tea. Why did she feel so weighed down with foreboding guilt over Lyle's drowning? *Was it an accident?* Perhaps that, too, was her mind playing tricks. Had Lyle deliberately abandoned her?

Meg always thought Lyle's secrecy was suspect whenever he went off on business trips in the past. Perhaps he really did have another woman and has gone to be with her for good.

Angela took Meg by the hand. 'Come and sit down—you look worn out. I guess anyone would, in your situation.'

Angela placed the food and coffee on a side table. 'I thought, before dinner, you might like to come with me for a walk along the beach—but have a rest first.' She handed Meg a cup of tea, followed by a plate with pikelets and jam.

'Yes, I'd like that. I haven't had much exercise since the upset with Lyle's disappearance. But please don't fuss over me. I can pull my weight while I'm here and I'd like to give you some money to contribute.'

Pete interjected. 'I wouldn't worry about that too much. Doubt whether you're going to eat us out of house and home.'

Meg smiled. She hadn't had this much show of love and care in years since before she married Lyle.

Pete's soft brown eyes searched her face. 'Make the most of it—you've had it rough for an awfully long time. We'll help you sort out your financial affairs too.'

Meg finished her tea and excused herself to take a nap. Her nerves were frazzled with so much change going on.

As she lay on the homely floral duvet surrounded by pleasant décor, gazing at Beth's paintings on the wall, she battled unwanted thoughts and fell asleep.

The bedroom door was slightly ajar when Meg awoke with Angela standing, checking on her. 'I'm sorry—I wasn't sure if you were awake, but it's getting late. You may not sleep well tonight if you have too much now.'

Meg jumped up and peered out the window. 'Oh, gosh, you're right. The sun has gone down. I'll just put my trainers on, and we could go for that walk.'

Meg welcomed her sister's warm-hearted company. Even Pete was similar—a proper gentleman, and she wondered why her sister could catch a prince when she married a toad—it wasn't fair.

After being couped up in the house for so long after Lyle's sudden disappearance, Meg relished breathing in the sea air and the leisurely stroll with Angela. The one thing she enjoyed about her life with a monster of a husband was her regular escapes to the beach near home. They gave her a reprieve from the enormous stress of living with a sociopath—a counsellor once told her, but Meg knew Lyle would often have a drone following her during those outings.

After they walked the length of the beach, Angela directed Meg to join her sitting on a park bench before heading back. She pulled a piece of dark chocolate from her jacket pocket and handed it to her.

'Here—get this into you. It's supposed to be good for your endorphins and give you a lift. I think you need plenty of that, right now.'

Meg grinned and grasped the chocolate.

'There's something I wanted to discuss with you and thought—at this stage—keep it between ourselves.'

Meg looked surprised and frowned at her.

'Oh—this sounds ominous. Is everything alright?'

'Not really. I'm concerned about you, Meg. I think you need help with this dilemma of yours.'

'What do you mean? If you are referring to Lyle leaving me—I'm glad he's gone, and hope he never returns.'

'No, not exactly. Something bad has happened that is disturbing you deeply. Pete and I both heard you yelling out in your sleep earlier. You were screaming and calling Lyle's name—saying the words *stay there and drown*!'

Meg's mouth dropped open as she paled.

'I must have been having one of those nightmares I was telling you about. It's so confusing.'

'Well, I can understand you have considerable contempt for that despicable man.

Anyone would have such thoughts or nightmares after what he put you through.'

Meg lowered her eyes. 'I certainly have held a great deal of resentment towards him.'

Angela stroked her hand. 'I can remember when you phoned me from Accident and Emergency for the first time years ago. The brute had almost broken your jaw.'

'Yes, it took a long time to heal, too. He never did that again though—I threatened to call the police. But after that, he started venting his narcissistic rage through psychological abuse instead,' she ranted, her voice shaking.

Angela wrapped her arms around Meg, whose eyes welled with tears. 'You're safe now. We'll help you get a top lawyer and obtain a restraining order.'

'Oh, please don't do that—I prefer not to involve the police just yet. He has gone, and I doubt if he'll be back. Leave it at the moment.'

'There is something else I want to ask you. I met someone who knew you years ago at St Andrews church when you and I were in the choir. Her name is Ann Grieves.'

Meg brightened. 'I remember Ann—that lovely detective. After her husband Terry got shot, I helped with the flowers for his funeral when I worked in the florist shop. That was shortly before I married Lyle.'

'That's right—she now runs her own business as a private investigator or detective, and I met her here last week shortly after you told me Lyle had gone missing. She can help you, as tracking unfaithful spouses is her specialty.'

'But you didn't tell her about Lyle, did you? I don't want the police involved—remember?' Meg's distraught face twisted with fear.

'I'm sorry, I had to do something—you were in a terrible state. Ann won't involve the police— not for something such as a deserting spouse. She and her partner, Tim, will track him down and see what he's up to.'

'What would that entail? It might enrage him more and make it worse.'

'Not with a restraining order. Anyway—she works under cover and won't do anything to put you in danger. It'll put your mind at rest if you know where he is.'

'So, what must I do—would I need to pay her up front?'

'No, you just have to drip feed her. But until we can get a lawyer to unlock the finances Lyle has tied up, we'll arrange legal aid for you.'

'What will Ann do first?'

'She asked for your consent to search your home for clues, if that's okay. You can tell her where you keep the spare key.'

'I guess that'll be alright. I don't care if I don't go back there. Once I get legal help to sell the house, I'll buy myself a cottage somewhere.'

'I think you're getting a bit ahead of yourself. In this situation, you won't be able to sell the house as your assets will be frozen while Lyle remains a missing person.'

'The swine—he still has control, even when we don't live together. He'll probably still haunt me when he's dead, too. I just can't escape him.'

Angela took her hand. 'You will be free—just be patient. He has only just gone missing. We'll get you a good lawyer, Meg. If you want to be rid of him completely, you'll need one.'

'Well, let's just see what Ann Grieves has to say about it all. Tell her where the spare key is hidden, so she can visit the house without either of us being there. The sooner this is sorted out, the better.'

Chapter Eight

Ann Grieves had just returned from taking her ex-police dog, Scout, for a walk on the promenade early in the morning, when she heard a familiar engine sound outside. Quickly unclipping the dog's lead, she hung it on the hook in the laundry. 'Come on, boy. I think we're in for a surprise.'

She opened the front door and commanded the dog to sit while she met her visitor at the gate.

'Tim! I thought you weren't due back from Australia until next week. You're up early—is everything alright?'

Ann hugged him. Even though he was only her nephew by marriage to her late husband, Terry, he was the son she'd never had.

'When did you arrive?'

'Flew in last night. I missed the drama back here, and both Mum and Dad had to return to work, which made it boring for me having to sit around all day until they came home each evening.'

'Well, you'd better come inside. I've been missing you. It's no good having our website posted all over the world as *Calamity Unlimited, Ann Grieves and Partner, Private Investigators,* if I don't have my partner in crime with me.'

Tim laughed as he walked into the lounge and sat himself down on her leather sofa.

'But you needed that break. I'm pleased you could get away for a while.' Ann leaned on the bench in her open-plan kitchen. 'Coffee, or a cool drink?'

'If you've got anything cold, that'll be great.'

'Sure—coming up.'

'I guess you've been running off your feet while I've been away?'

Ann brought the drinks into the lounge and handed him a bottle of Bundaberg ginger beer, knowing he didn't like to drink out of a glass. She poured herself a drink and sat down.

'Actually—things have been low key. I've only had a few wayward teenagers committing minor misdemeanours and someone running off with the takings from a church. But I think we're going to be involved in a more complex case.'

Ann explained to Tim the nature of the situation regarding Meg and her elusive husband.

'What do you think it is, Aunty? Just another case of an unfaithful spouse disappearing to be rid of his wife, perhaps.'

'No, I don't think so, but I smell a rat—something sinister going on. Her sister Angela phoned me last night and asked if I would investigate. She said Meg had given me permission to search her home. Now you're here, I'd like to go ahead as soon as possible.'

'Great—I'd love to get my teeth into something substantial. When do you want to go?'

'How about this afternoon? I don't want Meg to change her mind. She's staying with her sister in Woodlands by the beach and we can romp around the property while it's empty.'

Tim rubbed his hands together with delight. 'Can't wait.'

'Well—if you haven't anything else to do, we can go earlier if you like and then come back here for lunch.'

'Suits me fine.'

'I'm going to bring Scout. You know he's better at tracking than you and I put together and he has been begging me to give him some work to do.'

***

Ann pulled up in the driveway of a rustic home set on posts above the street level. It overlooked the beach with uninterrupted views—a piece of prime real estate.

She shivered. 'Ahh—someone just walked over my grave!'

Tim swung around and looked at her with surprise. 'What? That's a strange thing to say.'

Ann chuckled. 'I know—it's just an age-old saying meaning something spooked me and made my skin crawl.'

She leaned over and took Scout's lead from the back seat, clipped it to his collar and let him out.

'Come on, Tim. I'll look for the key first and hope it's where Angela said it would be. Can you hold Scout here for a minute?'

She scurried off up the footpath around the side of the house to the banana palm and searched the undergrowth at the base of the tree for a small jar. She found the key to the back door.

'Come on up here. I've got the key,' she called out to Tim. 'Let's have a good look around, and first, find his computer, or Meg's. You can usually discover a multitude of sins on those things.'

'Look at these, Aunty.' Tim pointed to the magnificent array of colourful butterflies mounted under glass on the wall of the room that must have been Lyle's office. There were also several photographs of the drone prototype that Angela had spoken of—how Lyle stalked Meg with them.

'Poor girl. Her sister talked about the brute's sadistic tendency to cause the butterflies to suffocate to death. They weren't, in fact, his— they were Meg's. She planted special shrubs and trees that attracted them and took delight in observing their beauty. They had brought her a great deal of joy, Angela told me.'

'He sounds like a right mongrel and I'm going to make sure we get him. He has to pay for the pain he brought her.'

Tim's compassionate heart melted Ann. That's what she liked about him most—his altruistic spirit.

She spotted a denim jacket lying on a chair in the bedroom that would likely fit a large man and stuffed it into a plastic bag.

'So, where do we go from here?' Tim asked when the house search delivered nothing.

Ann walked outside with him in tow, sensing Scout needed a tree where he could cock his leg.

'Hold on—I'll nosey around the garden while you search the garage and Lyle's wood-turning workshop.'

Ann handed Tim the key ring that held the remote for the garage. She took Scout and searched the garden for clues, exploring the small tin shed, and then rummaged around the fence, which was lined with a tall hedge.

'Come, Scout.' She bent down and held Lyle's jacket under the dog's nose. 'Good dog—go get a scent. Off you track.'

Scout's eyes lit up. His tail wagged frantically as he tugged hard on his lead.

Tim returned from searching the workshop. 'Nothing yet.'

'Let's follow Scout. He's been sniffing furiously and wants to lead me somewhere.'

'What—just around the garden? There's not much to explore here.'

'No—he wants me to go to the back of the property. There appears to be a well-trodden path up there through those trees.'

Tim glanced towards the forest. 'It just looks like a lot of bushes.'

'Trust me. My dog won't lead us astray—you should know that by now.'

They followed the exuberant Beagle through the back of the property onto the dirt path that led into a native forest. 'Mmm, I love the sweet smell of the earthy undergrowth. It has a kind of nostalgic appeal.' Ann inhaled deeply as they made their way after the dog.

Scout sniffed eagerly around the trees with the detectives in close pursuit until he stopped near the hollow log Meg had dumped there. He routed around it, whining and scratching at the soil, then sat still.

'Wait, Scout! Tim—help me drag this log away. He seems to think there's something underneath, and there is freshly dug soil.'

When they hauled the decayed tree trunk aside, Ann patted her canine friend on the head. 'Well done, boy.' She fished a small treat out of her pocket and gave it to him.

Ann always had rubber gloves stuffed into her jacket pockets and slipped her hands into a pair before bending down to study the soil.

'Put yours on too, Tim. I think we've got something.'

She shuddered at the thought of finding Lyle's body under the earth and tensed at the revelation that Meg could have killed her husband and buried him. Ann was in a quandary. How could she have moved him to the forest? There were no signs of dragging on the lawn or path. She must have used the heavy-duty wheelbarrow she saw in the garden next to the house.

'Tim—please trot down to the garden shed and bring a couple of spades.'

Before long, they had cleared away the debris Meg had placed over the burial site. As Tim dug deeper, Ann held her breath, thinking that any minute now a hand would appear protruding from the dirt.

After Tim had removed a vast amount of soil from the cavity that Meg had created, the contents of the grave lay bare, as they both stood staring at their uneventful find—a box containing fishing tackle, cell phone, laptop and dismantled fishing rods. Both their faces dropped with disappointment. No sign of a body.

Tim captured an image of their find with his phone. 'Why would anyone bury these items? Unless it was Lyle—before he left Meg.'

'It certainly is absurd.' Ann shook her head with a puzzled expression. 'We'd better put that soil back in there as best we can. This is going to be another baffling case. Perhaps you'll find some answers in the phone and laptop if they still function.'

They loaded the box of evidence into their vehicle. While Ann drove back to her house, she tried to work out a motive for anyone to hide those items. It just didn't make sense. If they belonged to Lyle, why wouldn't he take them with him? Perhaps he had something on the laptop that could incriminate him, and his wife found out.

'There's a case for us to solve, Tim. That's what you rushed back from Australia for, wasn't it? You won't be bored now. Perhaps our sweet Meg, the butterfly lady, is not so full of heart as she appears. We could have a murder suspect— and if her husband's body is not here, where is it?'

Chapter Nine

Meg was startled by a knock at the door. Her frayed nerves still electrified her, and she was reluctant to open it to see who was there and left that to Angela.

'Hello—I thought it might be you—come on in.'

Ann introduced Tim to Angela while Meg waited for them in the lounge, where they continued their greetings.

The sight of the waiflike creature she once knew as a vibrant, cheerful member of a church choir shocked her.

Meg stood biting her nails, still standing while everyone else sat down. Her pale face appeared to be exsanguinated—a ghostly white that made Ann shudder.

'It's good to see you, Meg. It's been a long time and I've never forgotten your kindness when I lost poor Terry.'

Meg managed to squeeze out a half-smile. 'Thanks, it was a sad time for you.'

'Angela has told me what you've been going through, and I thought you might like to hear a report of our findings when we searched your property. You won't like what we're about to tell you, but the sooner we get to the bottom of all this, the better for your health.'

Angela's face dropped, too. 'Oh dear, I hope it isn't too upsetting.'

'Well—no dead body or anything as macabre as that—but there was something.'

Meg slumped back on the couch next to Angela, wringing her hands and biting her lip.

'Tim's a cyber expert and a computer whiz. We always search out the PC and cell phone of any suspect. There we can find a can of worms, but in this case, we thought Lyle must have taken his digital devices with him—until we searched the forest behind the house.'

Meg stiffened. Her rigidity was noticeable by Angela. 'This must be disturbing for you. Are you alright?'

'Yes ... I think so. It has all been a bit much for me lately.'

Tim elbowed Ann on the couch where they sat together as she continued. 'My sure-footed Beagle dog led us up the back of the house and through a narrow dirt path to a group of trees. He began scratching under a hollow log, indicating to me there was something buried there.'

'That's strange,' said Angela. 'Where would he have got that scent if he is a sniffer dog.'

'Oh, I forgot to say I picked up what appeared to be a man's denim jacket from a chair in the bedroom and let Scout have a good sniff at it.'

All this time Meg had kept silent and then found her tongue. 'You mean your dog led you to the bush following Lyle's scent. Oh, no! Does that mean that he's buried there?'

Angela wrapped an arm around Meg's shoulders and held her close.

Ann chuckled and then realised the seriousness of the situation for Meg.

'No, there's no dead body up there, but what we found buried was what appeared to be Lyle's fishing gear, along with a few digital devices.'

She glared at Meg. 'Are you saying you know nothing about this? I'm wondering what your husband has to hide that he would go to such lengths.'

Meg didn't deny it outright, but just shook her head. 'It's bizarre—I'd love to know what else he's hiding.'

Ann wasn't sure how genuine Meg's answer was. It was as though she were concealing something.

She nodded at Tim. 'Well, I guess we'll find out more when we go through that laptop and cell phone we dug out of the ground. When we've finished, I'll be back to talk to you again, Meg.' Ann picked up her briefcase, ready to leave.

'Wait,' said Tim. 'We need the password for the laptop. Do you know what it is?'

Meg looked stunned, as though she was disassociating from them. 'Sorry—I don't know. He would never tell me anything like that.'

'Oh,' Tim said, grimacing. 'I'll give you a list of things that most people use if you can supply me with the information. If all else fails, we can take the laptop to a computer hardware expert to crack the password.'

'Do you mean like birthdays and names of his family?'

He and Ann sat down again.

Tim nodded. 'Yes—we'll start with birth dates, starting with yours and his, including family members.'

Meg reeled off a barrage of personal information before Ann left with Tim to head back to her home for a debriefing.

***

'We've got some digging to do, Tim,' said Ann, as she drove back to her house. 'And not in Meg's garden, but in Lyle's laptop and phone. I think we may be in for a few surprises and so will Meg.'

'Good! I need something to get my teeth into, otherwise I'll lose the touch.'

Ann chuckled. 'No chance of that, buddy. I think we may find this will not be a straight-forward case. There's a lot more to it than meets the eye, and I think Meg is deeply disturbed over something—not just an erring husband.'

'You don't think she has done him in or anything like that, do you?'

'I don't know—nothing surprises me about these situations with battered wives.'

'Where do we go from here ... I mean, apart from his digital devices?'

'Let's have something to eat and then I think we should go back to Langhome tomorrow and talk to a few locals—starting with the dairy owner. Perhaps they might shed some light on Lyle's whereabouts, or at least the last time anyone saw him.'

Tim rubbed his hands together. 'Sounds good to me. How about I start examining Lyle's devices after we've eaten?'

'Sure, you can do that—but I'm famished. Let me fix us a bit of lunch first.'

Chapter Ten

Ann was not keen on delaying their return to Langhome to interview the dairy owner and felt like taking the morning off. But in situations involving a missing person, investigators must work fast—it could mean life or death in some cases, of which she was well-acquainted.

Tim had arrived on his Ducati soon after Ann had finished her breakfast. He'd spent considerable time searching Lyle's laptop the previous evening—successfully guessing Lyle's password, which turned out to be a simple one—1935, his father's birthdate.

The majority of what Tim discovered on Lyle's computer were business files relating to his drone manufacture and the associated intellectual property rights. The man had appeared to have been a stickler for keeping everything under his control and had spreadsheets galore, including one for their household budget, which he appeared to micromanage.

Tim related to Ann that the amount of money Lyle had allowed Meg for her personal use was a pittance—if not an insult—nowhere near enough.

'Ah!' Tim stretched his arms—stiff after sitting up so late on the computer.

'So, the dirty dog must have a mistress hidden away somewhere.'

Ann yawned. Her brain had trouble absorbing so much information as she began to realise that this young man was far too quick for her.

She cautioned him about his eagerness to catch Lyle out. 'As I said—just because he has women's photos and corresponding phone numbers, it's not a crime and doesn't prove he's having an affair.'

'I still think it's so handy for him to go on these so-called business trips which Angela described to us.'

'You're right, Tim—that's the age-old alibi for straying partners. You'd better trace these women from his phone contacts to see who they are and compile a list for us for future reference.'

'Yeah—pity he's been cunning enough to delete his personal emails. I could only find business ones regarding his drone.'

'I thought Angela told us that he'd sold his drone prototype,' said Ann.

'Yes, he has—but remember she said he still assists the manufacturing company with training and testing support for customers.'

Ann nodded. 'Oh, yes, that's right. I'll have to check my notebook and see what I wrote about that.'

'I looked at his business records and it appears he receives royalties from his prototype. The company pays him for the training sessions he provides throughout the country.'

'I'm just about done in now, Tim, after all the running around yesterday. If I sit here much longer, I'll fall asleep—let's go.'

***

Kamal, the dairy owner in Langhome, was friendly enough. When Ann and Tim flashed their identity cards, he invited them to a comfortable sitting room at the back of the shop.

'Don't you need to watch in case someone shoplifts?' asked Tim.

'Nope—the buzzer goes off when anyone enters, and I have cameras in the shop.'

Ann made it clear to Kamal she wanted to keep their meeting with him confidential and that it would be in his own best interests.

'When did you see Lyle last, Kamal?'

'He and his wife came past here regularly—usually on a Friday before market day. The husband, Lyle, would catch fish to take there.'

'The last time Meg saw her husband was when they went fishing two Fridays ago. Is that the last day you spotted them too?'

'Oh, yes, that's right, Miss. I haven't seen either of them since the day I saw them both walking along the road towards Burns Point, but they didn't return together. Meg came back on her own just before sundown.'

'The lady often got cold or fed up, she used to tell me, and would leave her husband there and go back home.'

'Did you see either of them again that day?' asked Tim.

'No, sorry, I didn't. But I saw a light in the house last night as I was driving past, after I'd shut my shop. Just one dim glimmer in the lounge, as though all the lights were off except perhaps a lamp. I can't really see much though, as their house is above the road.'

Ann began taking notes. 'That's strange ... did you get to know the Doyles well at all?'

'No, not really ... there is something, though. Occasionally, the lady would pop into the shop for milk or bread, and twice she had black bruises on her arms. Another day, her face and one of her eyes were swollen. She always made excuses telling me she had another fall and needed glasses or tripped over the cat. But a neighbour said they don't have any pets. My wife Sunita has been quite concerned.'

'What are you trying to say, Kamal—don't you believe that's how she sustained the injuries?'

Kamal grimaced and reflected before he answered. 'I don't know, Miss—I'm not sure if she was telling the truth.'

'What about her husband, Lyle? Did he come down to your shop often?' asked Tim.

'Not often, but sometimes he came and asked me if I had seen his wife, or what time I saw her walking up the road. He was not a pleasant person—an angry sort of chap.'

Ann stood up. 'Thanks so much, Kamal, you have been more than helpful.' Ann handed him her business card. 'Please, would you contact me if you see Lyle or hear about any unusual activity regarding him? It appears he has gone missing.'

Kamal grimaced. 'Oh, dear.' He followed them out of the shop just as a customer entered.

'Thanks again. We'll be in touch.' Ann and Tim shook his hand and then left.

Chapter Eleven

'Come on, Tim. I'd like to go back to Meg's house and take another look around. Maybe our Mr Lyle Doyle is not missing after all. Let's check it out.'

Ann drove her car cautiously into the driveway, just in case there was another vehicle parked there already.

Tim stopped her, taking off ahead of him up the pathway to the house. 'Wait—what should we say if Lyle turns up?'

'After everything he has put his poor wife through, just tell him the truth. We're private investigators, and he's been reported as a Missing Person.'

'That's easy. I'd like to take a swipe at the mongrel if that's okay?'

Ann raised her eyebrows at him. 'You are joking, of course. We certainly don't want to be embroiled with the likes of him in a legal wrangle.'

'Don't worry, Aunty—it's just wishful thinking.'

They'd already had a key cut since their last visit to the house and went in through the backdoor.

To their surprise, it was as though the house had never been empty. On the dining table there was a half loaf of bread, margarine and a jam pot. There were even fresh crumbs on the wooden cutting board.

'Hey, Aunty—take a look at this.' Tim held a half-torn envelope and pulled out a document. 'Someone has been looking at this power bill. Lyle must be sneaking back here at night.'

'Weird—why would he do that,' Tim asked.

'In view of his sociopathic personality, it's possible he's been trying to drive Meg crazy and make her leave.'

Tim followed Ann along the hallway to the bedrooms. 'Look here—let me take a photo of this on my phone.' While Tim stood gaping, Ann took a snapshot of clothes carefully laid out on the King-sized bed that didn't appear to have been slept in.

'He must stay somewhere in the neighbourhood, or at least nearby. Either that, or he is a raging perfectionist. Come on—let's look down by the beach. I'd like to ask a few locals if they've seen him.'

'Good idea—but wait a minute. How about we install a miniature camera in here and make sure it is Lyle. If we show the recording to Meg, she can identify him.'

'Excellent! She has already given us consent to install surveillance cameras in and around the house,' Ann replied.

'He must use another vehicle. Once we know what he's driving, we can seize an opportunity to attach a small tracking device underneath the car.'

Ann chuckled. 'Wow—you've been watching that American police drama, NYPD Blue. Do you think you can install a camera on the bookshelf in the lounge too?'

Tim flushed. 'I know I'm a cyber expert, but that is a different kettle of fish. Although I'm not really familiar with video technology, I installed one for a neighbour, and it seemed to work okay. There's a Hi Fi store in the village.'

Ann locked the back door. They drove off down to the beach where there were several upturned dinghies and spotted a man busy sanding down an old kauri clinker. She pulled up beside him as he stopped to see what they were up to. Ann got out to speak to him.

'Looks like you have your work cut out for you there.' She smiled and stood gazing at the beautiful kauri wood he was restoring.

'Miles is my name,' he said, while Ann introduced herself.

After breaking the ice with small talk, she discreetly asked if he knew Lyle, expressing her concern that something had happened to him. It turned out that this man knew him well from the local fishing fraternity.

'I'm sure I saw him yesterday driving an old Ute with tinted windows. From the side view of the truck, I caught a glimpse of him through an open window. He usually drives a dated Peugeot, although I haven't seen it around for a while.'

'Well, thanks anyway. I'll have to get on my way now,' said Ann. 'Good talking to you—I appreciate your help.'

***

While they headed back to Ann's house, the two detectives swapped ideas on what they thought was going on between Meg and Lyle.

'He really is a sly dog sneaking around their home after driving Meg out. A crafty way of subtly getting rid of her,' said Tim, as though he had the case all sewn up.

'Here's another thought while you're at it, Tim. Perhaps it was Meg who arranged for someone else to go to her home and make it look as though Lyle had come back to taunt her.'

'What—now you're saying it could be Meg setting up her husband. Do you think she got rid of him?'

'Look—from what I know about battered women who've been psychological slaves for years—they can suddenly explode once they're at their wit's end. They've been known to fight back and seek revenge. Perhaps Meg has killed him and concealed evidence by hiding his laptop and phone to make it appear as though he was the one hiding something and had abandoned her.'

Tim nodded. 'You're right—in this business, nothing is ever as it seems. People often have ulterior motives.'

'And that's just it, Tim—it's all about motive. At the moment, however fragile and innocent Meg may appear, she has a compelling reason to make her husband suddenly disappear.'

Ann pulled into her driveway and parked in front of her garage. 'Now—do you want to stay for a bite to eat before you head off home?'

'Thanks, Aunty. I've already cleaned your fridge out, and I can see you're about to wilt. I've got a left-over Shepherd's Pie at home. That'll do me simply fine.'

'Can you purchase the cameras for Meg's house tomorrow? If you do that, I'll reimburse you, and the sooner we get that installed in the Doyle residence, the better. If it's Lyle who is acting covertly, we'll start tracking him. Get cams with an app that we can connect to both our phones.'

After Tim went home, Ann's head was spinning. It had been an eventful week. What seemed to be a simple case of an irritated husband wanting space from his marriage, this situation appeared to have a more macabre tone.

Scout had been at home all day, and Ann had no stamina left to take the poor animal for his daily walk. But it was a necessity, and this faithful, drug-sniffing champion had looked after her so well, it was time to reciprocate.

'Come on, boy, let's get a change of scenery.' She removed his lead from the hook and took him along the promenade, trying to settle her mind. The doctor's instruction to attend her swimming group at least once a week was not only good for her physical health but also for her mental well-being. It was completely forgotten in the hurly-burly of the case she and Tim were puzzling over.

Ann knew that with detective work, she had to keep a balance, but it was the nature of her occupation for everything to get thrown out of kilter. Most of the time it was organised chaos, but she loved the idea of fighting evil and for good to come out of that which was meant to harm her fellow man. It was her calling.

Chapter Twelve

Three Days Later

The phone app connected to the camera in Meg's home buzzed, causing Ann to startle. She fumbled around with the device, forgetting the instructions Tim had given her on how to use it.

'Confounded technology!'

Before she could decipher how to open the app and catch the culprit in action, her phone rang, which caused her to jump out of her skin again. She was relieved to see it was Tim calling.

'Man—am I pleased to hear you on the end of the phone. I guess you can see what I can't right now.'

'What? Can't you remember what I told you, Aunty. Press the red button and it will open up the camera—hurry!'

'Okay, just a minute.' Ann fumbled around for a moment but was afraid she would delete something and not be able to retrieve it.'

'Sorry, Tim. I'll have to wait till I see you. What's happening?'

'It's him ... Lyle. He's at Meg's house now. I know it's late, but can you pick me up? If we park somewhere nearby, we can get his car registration number. Please hurry.'

Ann was both elated and annoyed—vexed that she couldn't get her head around the new device on her phone—such a vital one at that. But also irritated that she couldn't have the early night she'd planned after a heavy day in the garden.

'Hold your horses, I'm coming now.'

She glanced at her watch. It was 9 pm. She quickly changed out of her pyjamas and on the way through the hall, grabbed her jacket and hat off their hooks.

Tim was waiting for her at his gate. She leaned over to open the car door for him.

'Thanks, Aunty. I hope he won't have gone when we get there. I'll keep the app open and watch what he's up to until we arrive.'

Tim explained to Ann on their way to Langhome the movement of Lyle, who behaved as though nothing was amiss while he was in the house. It was as though he was living his everyday life and had never gone missing.

'Don't worry, Aunty. I can download the recording onto my computer, and we can look at it later. Let's just get his vehicle details. I also have a mini magnetic GPS tracking device I purchased when I bought the camera. I'll attach it underneath his vehicle before he gets into it.'

Sure enough, there was an old Ute in the driveway. It seemed all so bizarre, Ann thought. *What was Lyle up to?*

She parked her car a little way down the street. They walked up the driveway to inspect the vehicle parked in front of Meg's garage.

Tim sprang up from behind Lyle's Ute. 'There you are—all done.'

'What do you mean?'

'The tracking device. It's all ready to go, inside the rim of his bumper.'

'My gosh—I can't keep up with all this—that didn't take you long. Thanks, Tim.'

They looked upwards and could see there was a dim light in the lounge, just as Kamal had said was the case, when he noticed someone had been at the house one night.

Ann whispered, 'We'd best only use the light from our phones—just in case he looks out the window or goes onto the deck—then we get out of here.'

Tim quickly captured a shot of the vehicle's registration details and they returned to Ann's car.

'What are we going to do now?' quizzed Tim, as he stepped back into the Land Rover.

'I don't think he sleeps there at night, although I'd like to know what on earth he is up to. I'm sure he's only leaving evidence of being alive and well for Meg's sake to frighten her. I guess we could wait and follow him. That's the best we can do for now.'

'He must be a real psycho to go to such lengths to torment his wife.'

'That's for sure, Tim—he's going to trip himself up—they always do.'

'So, we are going to just sit in the car and wait for him?'

'That's right. It's what private investigators do—surveillance work. We certainly earn our money. You don't have to be anywhere early in the morning, do you?'

'No, Aunty. I'm with you all the way. But now we can track him with that GPS.'

Ann handed him a chocolate protein bar. 'Here—I keep these on hand for situations like this and grabbed them from the fridge before we left. They always help when the adrenaline is running high.'

'Gee, thanks. At least it's a warm night—I wouldn't fancy sitting for hours in the cold.'

Ann chuckled. 'Harden up, Mister. That might happen on occasions. I want to follow him if he's staying in the neighbourhood and find out more about his activities and who he's in league with.'

They sat watching Lyle's movements in the lounge and open-plan kitchen, which was the only area the camera could reach. He sat watching the TV—now and then, ducking into the fridge for a beer or something to eat. After disappearing up the hallway, he returned to the lounge with a small travel bag then switched the lights out. He locked the door and left the house.

'Hey, listen!' Tim wound down the window. He picked up his phone and checked the surveillance app. 'He has hopped into his Ute. I also fixed a mini camera on a tree opposite the car, which can detect the whole driveway. Let's follow him.'

They waited until the Ute had gone round the corner on the narrow, windy road that twisted its way along the beach. Then they followed. They drove past Lyle's fishing spot at Burns Point, and a little further down the road, Lyle turned off into a side road, pulling up in the driveway of someone's home.

Ann parked a short distance away. They hurried on foot to the gate of the property he had entered, where Ann noted on her phone the street address as they hid behind a hedge. Another vehicle was parked in a carport. Men's voices and laughter echoing across the lawn broke the stillness of the night, as a man appeared on the doorstep greeting Lyle.

'What have you done this time? You're becoming the master of deception. Perhaps you should join the movies.' They laughed again and continued their banter as Lyle entered the house.

'So, that's it. He's been hiding out here—all the while making out that he was dead or had gone missing—giving his wife hell. And yet, he's not breaking the law. He has every right to go and stay with a friend and come and go to his home at every whim.'

Tim let out a long sigh. 'How are we going to sort this out, then? All our efforts have been in vain.'

'Not at all,' Ann said swiftly. 'There is much more to this man than meets the eye. He has something to hide. Or he wouldn't bother going to such lengths—doing what I said before—

deliberately sending his wife over the edge. There is something we have missed, as I mentioned earlier.'

They walked back to the car. 'I'll drop you off home—let's get some sleep and start again in the morning. It's getting riskier now that Lyle is visiting the house, but we need to search his workshop thoroughly next time, where he does his woodturning.'

'Why is that Aunty?'

'That's where I think we've missed something. From my experience, with criminals who've had *man caves* at home, they think they are the last place anyone would look for evidence, but that's the first place we usually find it. I should have helped you search there that day. I've an inkling we may find a clue there.'

After Ann had dropped Tim home, she received a text message from Angela who asked to call her in the morning.

Chapter Thirteen

Ann returned from her early morning walk with Scout, famished. She hadn't eaten much the evening before and felt like spoiling herself with bacon and eggs.

She finished the meal, washing it down with a mug of coffee then remembered Angela's message to phone her.

'Hi, Angela. How is Meg? I have some news for her, but I'll pop around this morning with Tim, if that's okay.'

The voice on the other end of the phone sounded agitated. Meg had not been doing too well—still having frightening nightmares. The counselling sessions they'd arranged for her didn't seem to work. Angela ranted as Ann listened intently.

'Until Meg finds out what happened to Lyle, there's not much hope of her healing.'

Taking a deep breath, Ann jumped in. 'That's what I want to talk to her about. We've fresh news regarding Lyle, but I'll discuss it when we come tomorrow—late morning.'

Ann came off the phone, anxious about how she was going to approach Meg with news about Lyle. It wouldn't be safe for the woman to return home soon but would have to collect the rest of her belongings, eventually.

Picking up her mobile again, Ann contacted Tim to warn she'd meet him at his gate. She also mentioned the discussion she would have with Meg.

After collecting him at the end of his driveway the next morning, Ann discussed the plan for the day as they drove off to see Meg.

'I'd like to visit Meg's property for the last time and see what we can uncover in Lyle's workshop—I'm leaving no stone unturned.'

'What will you say to him if he arrives while we're rooting through his workshop? He could go ballistic.'

'It's okay, Tim. We must stay calm and say that Meg has reported him as a missing person and hired us as private investigators.'

'I'll feel like punching him on the nose if I see him.'

Ann's brows knitted together. She glared at him.

'You won't do anything of the kind! That's one of my rules while working with me. If you start swinging your fists around, it'll ruin my business. Your job is to stay cool at all times. That's how you win—unless its self-defence, of course.'

'I get you—sorry, Aunty, I was only venting my absolute contempt for a wife beater. They're cowards.'

Ann was pleased to see Tim expressing his emotions and showing sensitivity towards a battered woman, but the last thing she needed for her business and reputation was a lawsuit for grievous bodily harm, or GBH, as she called it.

'Were you able to identify the owner of Lyle's Ute? You said you would look up the registration number.'

'Oh, yes—I forgot to tell you. It's registered under his name, Lyle Doyle. He must have bought it straight after he split from Meg.'

'He doesn't waste any time. He probably bought it off that mate he is staying with.'

Ann drove tentatively down the street leading to the Doyle's home, making sure the notorious Ute wasn't parked in the driveway before pulling up in front of the garage.

Tim jumped out and raced up the back of the property to Lyle's workshop with Ann in close pursuit, trying to remember where he had searched there the first time he'd looked. What stone had he left unturned?

Ann joined him and sensed his hesitation.

'Remember when we rummaged around the house belonging to that security officer from Softsculpt during our previous case? The hot items were hidden in false panels, cupboards and drawers. That's what we have to hunt for now.'

'I was just thinking exactly that, Aunty. This is Lyle's cave, and someone like him is bound to be hiding a hornet's nest.'

A short while later, they couldn't find any false drawers or sliding panels, and as they were about to give up on their search, Ann stopped in the doorway.

'Wait—I recall finding contraband hidden in a woodturners workshop once, under his workbench.'

'Excellent thinking, Aunty!'

Tim looked underneath the workbench where the wood lathe stood. 'No, nothing there,' he said, pulling his head back up from underneath the ledge.

'Ah, just as I thought.' He looked again closely at the workbench. 'Can you help me to lift the lathe onto that table over there, please, Aunty? I don't think it'll be too heavy with the two of us.'

Ann frowned. 'Now what are you up to?'

'Please just help move it and I'll show you.'

Ann could see the benefit of her swimming and gym training when she lifted the large piece of machinery—not as unfit as she thought.

Once they were done, Tim lifted the flip-top lid of the bench. 'See this—it was designed to look as though the top was in one piece, but I could tell from the sizeable built-in cavity that there was more to it than meets the eye. It would hardly conceal contraband or drugs from the police, but it's a compartment to hide secret documents from a spouse.'

There were, just as Tim had guessed, hidden items. As Ann peered over his shoulder, he removed the rubber band holding a stack of envelopes. The correspondence was obviously from a lover and consisted of letters tucked inside birthday and Christmas cards.

Ann had expected to find drugs or something as incriminating, but perhaps these might provide them with a few answers to Meg's dilemma, she hoped.

'The man's such a dark horse, and this case gets more complicated the further we dig,' said Ann.

Tim flicked through a bunch of letters. 'Shall we take a look at these before we head over to see Meg? Then we can tell her the whole story—at least, of what we've learned about her covert husband.'

'Absolutely. We'd better move, though. We can park down by the beach.'

'Wait, Aunty. We'd better shift the lathe back to its original place on the workbench. Can you give me a hand with it please?'

They left the property and drove down to a pull-in by the beach. As they rummaged through the mail, it was just as Ann had thought—love letters.

Tim's eyes narrowed as he quickly scanned the addresses on the back of the enveloped.

'They are postmarked Brisbane and were sent to a post office box in Langhome by someone called Eddie Thorpe—but that's a man's name.'

Ann was still busy sifting through the rest of the letters. 'It's hard to believe he has a man as a mistress. We'll have to give these to Meg. She instructed us to search her property, so that covers us if we hand it over to her.'

'No, wait! What are the dates on the postmarks? Maybe Lyle received these before he met Meg.' Tim fingered through the envelopes. 'Look here—you told me Meg married him after Uncle Terry's funeral. But these were written long before that.'

Ann inspected the postage dates. 'You're right, but he must have been quick off the mark latching onto Meg so soon after leaving Eddie.'

'What do we do about Lyle now?' Tim asked, animated by the intrigue.

'We need to follow him and hope he'll lead us to his lover. Can you do an image search with that background app you have on your computer?'

'Yes, but it's not completely accurate. Especially with women who can change the colour and style of their hair so easily—but I'll try. I reckon our best bet is to track him when he hopefully pays her a visit.'

'Tim, we can't keep the surveillance cameras in Meg's house, I'm afraid—now that Lyle is no longer missing and living back there.'

'What? But he's not sleeping at the house— he's just pretending to live there.'

'It's against the law to stalk anyone with a video camera in the privacy of their home. When Meg wanted them installed and needed to know if her husband was living there, it was allowable. But now that we are watching him on your app, I think we could get into trouble legally—and believe me, that husband of Meg's would go the total distance to incriminate us.'

Tim's face dropped. 'After all that—what a confounded waste of time. What about the tracker in his vehicle?'

Ann hesitated in deep thought. 'If Lyle owns that Ute, it will make it relationship property, and it wouldn't be illegal for Meg to have a GPS tracker attached to it. People use them in case their vehicles are stolen.'

'Good—that gives us an out to continue following him,' said Tim, with a smug expression on his face.

'Good work. Even if we find he has a lover somewhere, it's not incriminating evidence. But it may convince Meg to divorce the monster and start a new life.'

Tim unwrapped a piece of chewing gum. 'What shall we do with these letters? We don't want Lyle to know we've discovered his floosie in Australia.' He popped the gum into his mouth.

'I was just coming to that. We have to put them back, but I want you to photograph a few which may be pertinent to this case. Let's go.'

They raced back up the hill to the Doyle's home again. In no time at all, with Ann's help, Tim replaced the cards and letters in the secret compartment of the lathe bench, having already taken snapshots of some of them while in the car. They were in and out of there in a flash, relieved Lyle had not returned to the house during both of their visits.

'Whew! That was a lucky break, wasn't it, Aunty? I just imagined him walking in and seeing us reading his secret love letters. He would have come at us like a wounded bull.'

Ann was amused and chuckled. 'I didn't want to say, but I thought we were going to have a right confrontation with him at any moment but thank God he must have been out fishing or somewhere. He obviously only comes to the house at night so he can remain covert.'

'You and I make a good team, don't we?' Tim looked at her for approval.

'You can count on that, partner. Who would have thought I'd be fighting crime with Terry's nephew? It's a strange old world.'

Chapter Fourteen

Ann pulled into Angela's driveway. A face appeared at the lounge window—it was Meg.

She answered the door—this time, wide-eyed but not bushy-tailed. Her demeanour was flat and there was barely any colour in her cheeks, Ann noted. Perhaps today's news might give her face a rosy flush.

Angela directed them all to take a seat at the dining table. Tim placed his laptop down, ready to show Meg the camera recording.

Ann wasn't sure whether the news she was about to give Meg would enthral or upset her— she still had doubts about whether she was telling the truth.

'Do you have news about Lyle?' she asked, her voice quavering.

'Yes, dear, we have. I'm not sure whether it's good or bad news for you. Especially if you were hoping your abuser had disappeared for good. I'm afraid Lyle is alive and well—still living in your neighbourhood.'

Meg's face turned white again. 'What do you mean living in the neighbourhood—you mean he's back home?'

'Well, no, not exactly. We placed a surveillance camera in your house and driveway. Tim can show you what we saw.'

He opened up the recording of Lyle at the house. When Meg saw him sitting in the lounge watching TV as though nothing untoward had taken place, she was furious.

'Cunning monster—he isn't even dead ... I mean he hasn't disappeared, after all!'

With that outburst, the detectives' eyes met, both sharing the same thoughts.

Ann's icy stare penetrated Meg, who'd realised the detective had caught on to what she'd mistakenly blurted out.

'Meg—what made you think Lyle was dead? I thought you said he'd abandoned you.'

She froze, searching frantically for an answer. 'I meant missing—I said disappeared. But for all we know he could have been dead and so I was confused.'

Ann's eyes narrowed. 'Are you sure you are telling us everything that happened the day Lyle made you angry, and you smashed the butterfly jar?'

'I didn't tell you that, did I?'

Meg began to fidget with her wedding ring.

'No,' said Ann. 'But Angela told us what happened to your beautiful blue butterfly and that you couldn't take it anymore. You smashed the jar, and Lyle made you stay down on your knees until you'd picked up all the glass fragments, causing your finger and knee to bleed. If that were me, I'd be at my wit's end too.'

'I told you I left him there fishing that afternoon, as I was cold. Lyle was being his usual nasty self. I just couldn't cope anymore and stalked off home. I hated him for what he did.'

This time Angela began questioning her in front of the detectives. 'What about the nightmares, Meg? They are repetitive and you often call out in the night. Sometimes you scream in your sleep and I get up to see if you are alright. You keep yelling *Lyle is drowning* and *my butterflies are free now.*'

Ann was taking down every word in her day book.

'Meg—tell us what really happened that day. Something traumatic has occurred for you to get into this state. Lyle is alive and hasn't disappeared. But he is definitely up to something, and we want to make sure you come out on top.'

'Yes, we're here to help, not incriminate you,' said Tim warmly.

Meg pushed her face into her hands as an avalanche of tears cascaded down her pale cheeks. Angela handed her a box of tissues. Meg clutched a handful and honked into them.

The three looked at each other and waited. Angela took her hand. 'Please, Meg. You want to get well, don't you? We can't go on like this. These people are on our side—trying to help you.'

Between deep sobs, Meg poured out half the truth.

'Lyle had become meaner and meaner—controlling to the extent I was a prisoner in my own home. When I took my artwork to the market each Saturday, women there would tell me how eventful their lives were and all the interesting things they were doing. The part that hurt most, was when I saw them out and about with their little ones—happy families having the life I couldn't, as Lyle denied me children and I knew he didn't like them.'

Meg stuffed the used tissues into the pocket of her jeans and took another handful, still blubbering between paragraphs, as she took quick breaths while Ann continued to write, barely able to keep up.

'I ... haven't been entirely honest about what happened the last day I saw Lyle—when we went fishing together.'

Ann stopped writing, her mouth dropping open as her eyes fixated on Meg's every word.

Angela took her hand and squeezed it. 'Are you sure you should talk right now? You are still in shock and not completely recovered.'

Meg smiled at her. 'It's okay. I can't hold on to this any longer.'

Between sobs, she told how Lyle had bullied her so much the day he captured her magnificent blue butterfly. When he put it inside a preserving jar, she smashed the vessel—as she just couldn't tolerate his abuse any more. The tension had been building up in their marriage for the past year, and the extent of Lyle's sadistic torment escalated—so much that Meg hated him and secretly wished him dead.

Ann flashed Tim a glance, raising her eyebrows.

'The last time I saw him, was that afternoon we went fishing. He treated me like a slave as usual—but more so that day because I set his prized butterfly free. He was in a rage, and while he stood on the rock bellowing at me—giving orders—I was tempted to push him into the water, as I knew he couldn't swim.'

Angela glared at her with a horrified expression.

'Is that what you did?' said Ann. 'Push him into the sea?'

'No, wait! I wanted to—that's what he deserved. But as he turned to shout at me to bring him more bait, a huge wave scooped him off the rock and dropped him into the tide.'

'So, you tried to rescue him?' Tim asked.

'No, I didn't. As he floundered around in the waves, I couldn't move—my feet seemed to stay glued to the ledge where I stood. He kept screaming at me to pick up his spare rod and give him one end then pull him up.'

Angela sat, shaking her head in disbelief. 'Couldn't you do that?'

'As I said, my body wouldn't move. An inner voice kept saying to me, *save him and lose your own life*. I knew that if I pulled him out, I would spend the rest of my life in a living hell.'

Angela rubbed Meg's arm to comfort her. 'He didn't deserve to live.'

Ann nodded at Meg. 'Please continue—what happened, then?'

'As he began sinking and his head started ducking under the water, I turned and walked away home. Ever since then, I've been having these terrible flashbacks and nightmares, reliving the whole thing all over again. I believed he drowned.'

'But you didn't kill him,' said Angela. 'It's not your fault.'

Tim had also taken notes. 'Was it you who buried his laptop and phone with his fishing gear in the forest behind your house?'

'Yes, it was. I felt guilty, as though I'd killed him, because my contempt for him had been so strong. I was afraid I would get arrested for murder, so I constructed a plan to make it appear as though he had suddenly deserted me.'

Ann flashed her a sympathetic glance. 'Well, it was a clever plan and almost believable, until he turned up at your home again.'

Angela's face turned red with anger. 'So that rotten pig is still alive and living carefree in their marital home after driving Meg out—how can that be?'

'It's not as straightforward as that. Lyle may be up to something which needs further investigation—apart from tormenting you, Meg. There's something else we have discovered. Tim can tell you about that.'

Ann's side-kick leaned forward, resting his elbows on his knees, looking up at Meg.

'Do you know a friend of Lyle's called Eddie? This is someone who has sent him frequent letters. Under his workbench that holds the lathe, there is a false drawer made to appear as part of the base of the bench. Inside I found these endearing birthday and Christmas cards with old love letters, all dated long before he met you.' Tim handed Meg a couple of letters he'd kept as proof before placing the rest back inside Lyle's workbench. Meg's eyes bulged as they studied the intimate writings of her brute of a husband to another woman.

'What—it must have been an old flame of his?' She handed them to Angela, who quickly scanned mail.

'There is a heap more in his secret drawer. I only brought these as confirmation he was going to marry this woman in Australia,' said Tim.

'Eddie's a man's name though, short for Edwin or Edward. Do you think he was in a gay relationship, or maybe still is?' The date of the postmarks is way before my time,' Meg mumbled.

'Bizarre,' muttered Angela.

'No, it's possible that Eddie is short for Edwina, but we aren't sure.'

'We need to continue to track Lyle when he's driving around in his Ute and hope he leads us to Eddie's address so we can identify her or him. She probably lives close by, and if she moved over here from Australia, Lyle has been shrewd or stupid enough to continue seeing her while married to you,' said Ann.

Meg looked as though she was going to pass out.

'Are you okay? I'll get you some water.' Angela hurried off to the kitchen. She returned with a glass and continued trying to console her.

'Meg—we're going to get off now, so we'll be ready for Lyle once he leaves the neighbourhood. We'll check what he's up to and catch him out—don't you fret.'

'Now, that explains his so-called weekend business trips to Australia. He was probably cavorting with this woman in Queensland and now she has moved here!' Meg was all cried out, and Ann could see signs of relief in her face now the police couldn't charge her with getting rid of husband. But there was now another investigation on the way.

'Thank you both for all you've done in uncovering Lyle's whereabouts. I was getting sick with worry that I may have killed him in a blackout.'

Angela put an arm around her. 'I think we'd better take you home and help you clear out your things. You can't stay there with that monster hanging around. We'll find you an excellent lawyer to sort this out.'

Meg grabbed a handful of paper tissues from the box Angela had placed next to her and blew her nose loudly.

'Sorry, ladies, but we really need to get going. I'll be in touch once we have more information about Lyle's movements. Please phone me or Tim if you have any further information that may help with our investigation.'

Chapter Fifteen

Late the following morning, Ann and Tim sat at the dining table mulling over the scene that had taken place with Meg at her sister's house. Tim tapped his pen repetitively on his notebook and stopped when Ann gave him her disapproving look.

'Thanks for lunch, Aunty—it's my turn next.'

'Okay, I'll hold you to that.'

'I was thinking—what if Meg really tried to knock Lyle off when they were fishing that day? He could have deliberately faked his death to get back at her. She may even try to have another shot at getting rid of him.'

Ann shook her head. 'Now, Tim. I think you're letting your imagination run away with you. It's the other way around, I'd say. Lyle would want to take revenge for the humiliation she caused him and for his lack of control when he almost drowned.'

Tim shrugged his shoulders. 'I guess so.'

'Oh—I forgot to say I phoned and explained to Meg that we can't continue camera surveillance legally inside her home any longer. Now that Lyle is living back in the house, it would be seen as an invasion of his privacy without his consent, and we would not be able to access it as evidence.'

Tim grimaced. 'But I thought that Meg had given her consent.'

'That was only while her husband was believed to be missing, and she wanted to know who had been in her house at night.'

'Well, that's a let down!'

'Meg said she would ask Pete to remove the cameras and give them back to us, as he and Angela were there with a trailer, helping her shift her stuff out when I rang. Just imagine the showdown if Lyle had walked in.'

'I certainly can.' Tim chuckled. 'There's not much we can do after this, except wait until we can start tracking Lyle's movements in his Ute.'

'Where has the vehicle been today—did you see anything suspicious?'

'Nothing—only a short trip he made into the village and back to his friend's house,' said Tim.

'Perhaps he's lying low since he rattled the hornet's nest by driving Meg away. Don't worry—he'll drop himself in it sooner or later. You mark my words.'

***

Tim had not seen much activity with Lyle's Ute—apart from a few trips to his home at night. On Friday evening, the tracking app on his Ute indicated that he was taking a longer trip than usual.

Tim stopped what he was doing on his computer and pulled on a pair of boots and his leather jacket. He grabbed his helmet from the chair in his office and darted off around the side of the house to his Ducati.

He was relieved it was a warm spring evening, as he didn't relish riding his bike at night in the cold. Although he was an avid motorcyclist, he often wondered if it was time he bought himself a car for his detective work, but the motorcycles also had great attributes for investigative work.

On the vehicle tracking app, Tim could see Lyle was driving along the narrow coastal road that would eventually lead to the main highway. He would have to get to the turnoff to the motorway before Lyle and track him from there with his own GPS.

'Darn,' he muttered, as the Ute headed off on State Highway East, which meant Tim could have a long night ahead of him. He followed close behind Lyle as his vehicle turned off towards the South Eastern side of the city. Twenty-minutes later, the Ute branched off towards Clovelly Heights near the towering cliffs and eventually pulled into a driveway.

Tim drove straight past, did a full circle around the block and returned to where Lyle's vehicle had come to a standstill. He parked his motorcycle under a tree and ducked behind a shrub in the driveway—just in time to see Lyle in a loving embrace kissing a woman standing next to a stately Queenslander house. Lyle removed an overnight bag from his car boot and took the woman's hand as they wandered inside the house together.

'Sly dog—just as I thought,' Tim mumbled, as he perceived the young woman would have been nearly half Lyle's age. Frustrated there was nothing more he could do—he noted the address on the letterbox on the way back to his bike.

Tim felt a huge sense of achievement, knowing his partner would be pleased at his discovery. Now the waiting game had begun, as they were able to monitor Lyle's movements and see how long he spent with this new woman. But most of all to find out who she was and whatever background information he could gather about her. He was now as keen as Ann was about finding enough dirt on this serial abuser to incriminate him. Lyle deserved to pay for all the damage he caused Meg.

Tim was now on a mission to discover the identity of the woman at the Clovelly address he visited. Was she the one called Eddie—or some other floosie of Lyle's—perhaps one amongst many?

The following afternoon, Tim was on the phone to Ann with the results of his research on the woman at the address Lyle had visited the previous night.

'It's not the mysterious Eddie, I'm afraid. The woman is Patty Gregg—in fact, I remembered seeing her name amongst Lyle's phone contacts listed as a journalist. The background search says she is twenty-eight years old and born in Dunedin. I'd love to know how Lyle meets these women.'

'Think about it, Tim. He's a travelling businessman and has every opportunity to covertly meet females.'

'I guess we don't know how long he's been going with Patty—he may have only just met her.'

'Well, we can keep those two under surveillance, but what about Eddie—the one who said in the many cards we read that he was the love of her life?'

Chapter Sixteen

Ann and Tim visited Meg without warning with news about Patty Gregg, hoping she could shed some light on this new discovery.

Relieved to find her home, Ann spotted her peering out the window before she opened the door to them.

'Hello—you're back again.'

This time Ann felt Meg was much more confident, as though she was free of her Acute Stress Disorder, which Angela had discussed with her. She'd explained that it was a type of Combat Fatigue, an accurate description for the situation Meg had been in with Lyle.

Meg gathered them around the dining table again as Angela entered the room from the kitchen.

'We have a lot of work to get through today. Tim has some more news—unpleasant, I'm afraid, but you need to know about this and help us with our investigations.'

Tim elaborated on his tracking adventure following Lyle's Ute and what he saw when he arrived at Patty's address.

Meg clasped her hand over her mouth. 'Oh, no. Poor girl, we have to warn her—otherwise she's going to suffer the way I did.'

Ann patted her hand. 'We have to get our facts right first and make sure she isn't some relative of Lyle's and that it isn't a perfectly legitimate relationship.'

Meg handed Ann a document. 'I've got some news, too. When I was at the house moving all my stuff out, there was this letter in the mailbox for me. I'm the only one who receives post at home. Lyle uses a private lobby box for business—or so he says.'

Ann peered over the brim of her glasses. 'It's from Lyle's lawyer. It looks like you're going to be completely set free if you wish. Lyle wants to stay in the house and buy you out but doesn't mention anything about paying you half of his drone business—you're entitled to that.'

'He has the audacity to say I can set myself up somewhere in a little flat, thinking he's doing me a favour by driving me out of my own home and then offering me the pickings.'

Angela reacted to Meg's ranting and came and sat next to her to calm her down.

'I told you, Meg—we are going to get a powerful lawyer to deal with this—our fellow will not let you down, and we'll make sure you get a fair settlement. You can't go back to that house. Once it's all over, you'll be completely free.'

Ann gave Meg a sympathetic smile. 'Your sister is right. Please take her advice and get this letter to a lawyer to complete. You'll be able to start a new life—a happy one at that.'

'I hear you all. What was the name of that woman, Patty, again? Write it down for me, please, Tim—and her address.'

Ann had doubts about why Meg was so keen to note down Patty's details. What did she have up her sleeve? But Tim handed it to her, as he thought it the right thing to do.

The two detectives excused themselves and promised to be in touch if they gathered any more dirt on Lyle. It was certainly piling up, and it appeared he may not only be a wife beater, but it was dawning on them that he was also a serial adulterer. If he was that unscrupulous, what else lay at the bottom of that can of worms?

***

111

Ann felt guilty for neglecting Scout. It had been a hectic week, and she didn't enjoy not having any time to herself. While working on a case, she was determined not to leave any stone unturned.

When she was in the police force, there were always others who could take the flack. But these days—even with Tim onboard—it was still not that easy to take a break. Because of the amount of internet work required for investigations, he was barely able to assist Ann with physical tracking of suspects and surveillance activities.

'Come on, Scout—let's get out of here.' She attached the lead to his collar and headed off down the promenade.

After a long walk and before heading back to the house, Ann sat on the park bench where she usually rested to watch the waves lapping into the shore. Her heart somersaulted— someone tapped her on her shoulder.

'Ann! You're a hard one to pin down. I haven't seen you around here for a while with that pooch of yours. Is everything okay?'

It was Ted, one of her neighbours who always knew everything that was going on in her community.

'Oh, hi, Ted. I've been fine, thanks. Just caught up in my work.'

'I heard all about that—the missing man—Lyle Doyle. Has he been found yet?'

Ann tensed. 'Sorry—what did you say? Lyle Doyle—how did you hear about that?'

'I was talking to my fishing mate, Miles, a few days ago. He told me you spoke to him when he was on the beach sanding down his boat and asked if he'd seen Lyle Doyle around. You said he'd gone missing, but Miles had seen him driving a Ute in the area, instead of his Peugeot.'

Ann cleared her throat. 'Oh—did I say that? I think Mr Doyle is alive and well.'

'Miles knows all the fishermen in the area—I guess he'll find out what's going on.'

Scout came running as his mistress called out to him.

'Sorry, Ted, but I have to get going. I'll catch up with you another day.'

She was worried now and should have known living in a small coastal area that word travelled fast—Langhome was not that far from Cockle Cove. Of course, Lyle would find out that she'd been digging—and what else did he know about their investigations?

Ann had convinced herself there was nothing wrong with her course of action, as Angela had reported Lyle as missing initially. He could have been dead, for all Meg knew, even though it had turned out not to be the case.

Ann also realised, fortunately for her, that Pete had removed the surveillance cameras from the house, otherwise she could have had a lawsuit on her hands. Lyle would have been livid over Meg having a hired private investigator to track him down.

Chapter Seventeen

A week later

'Calamity Ann—where have you been all this time? I haven't heard from you since the Softsculpt case.'

Ann was on the phone calling her friend Detective Inspector Bryce Drummond, now a senior member of the Criminal Investigation Bureau stationed at the Cockle Cove Police Station. He was one of the few people who still addressed Ann as Calamity—a nickname from her days in the police force.

'I had another case pretty much on the heels of my previous one, and I've been up to my eyeballs in it. No time for socialising.'

'No problem—how can I help?'

'I don't exactly need your assistance—not yet at least. But I'd love you to come for dinner this Saturday evening—if that suits.'

'Mmm, this sounds ominous. But you know me. Any chance of somebody else's cooking and I'm in—especially yours.'

Ann was thinking Bryce had always been a bit of a charmer. He'd never really got over the death of his wife, just as Ann still hadn't moved on from her beloved Terry's death after he was shot in a police ambush. She was glad that this DI still looked out for her, as the life of a widow could sometimes be lonely—although Ann did have her nephew to fuss over.

'Can you come at around six? It'll give me plenty of time to prepare. I'm getting out of practice these days,' she humoured.

After speaking to Bryce, Ann was about to put her phone back in her pocket when it vibrated and rang loudly. It was Tim who had been busy at home, where he carried out all his online research for Ann.

'I've found some background information about this Eddie person who sent Lyle those love letters. I went on a hunch that she may be involved somehow with the manufacturing company which produces his drones. Starting in Brisbane, Australia, where Lyle's factory was first located, I conducted a search on that organisation. Edwina Thorpe is listed as being contracted as freelance Conference and Events Manager.'

Ann couldn't believe her luck. 'You've got to be kidding—are there any photos of her?'

'Yes—but this was several years ago, and she appeared a great deal younger than Lyle would have been back then.'

'Would you mind sending the information through to me on our secure portal—and anything else you can dig up? If you can track her whereabouts—that would be even better. I've got to go out for a few hours, and after I've seen the background information on Edwina you're sending me, I'll phone you.'

Ann was relieved to finish the call, but she also felt elated by the fresh breakthrough. Although she was tempted to turn off her phone altogether to give herself a rest, she was afraid that it would be just at the wrong moment.

It was time to head off to the leisure centre and swim a few lengths—doctor's orders. Despite her occasional midnight snacking, her weight had begun to decrease. She was beginning to get stiff, sitting around each day either on her laptop, interviewing people or driving her Land Rover.

To her delight, the gym was almost empty at that time of day, and although she loathed working out and would rather swim, she always tried to warm up by doing five minutes on the rowing machine and a few weights before progressing to the swimming pool.

Back in the change-room again, she pulled on her modest bathing costume and glanced in the mirror before tiptoeing out to the pool. As she walked down the ramp, the tepid water soothed her. She planned to swim several lengths and then sit in the spa pool.

It was later than Ann thought when she glanced at the large clock on the wall after being mesmerised by the bubbles in the spa. It was time to get out, as she'd promised Tim to check their private investigators' portal and give him further directions but had almost fallen asleep.

***

'What else were you able to get while I was away, Tim? I'm betting that Edwina Thorpe is our Eddie—he sure likes them young.'

'Just like that girl Patty I saw him with. Naïve and vulnerable, I guess.'

Ann felt her heart race in hopeful expectation of possibly cracking another case. 'You're right, Tim. So, let me have it—what else?'

'I reckon this piece of information deserves another meal in the Jolly Roger restaurant—your shout, of course,' he said, chuckling.

'I might just do that—cheeky thing.'

'Found an address for Edwina Thorpe who lives south of Brisbane on the Gold Coast near Dreamworld.'

'Are you thinking what I'm thinking, Tim? I guess I'm about to fund a trip for you to the Gold Coast to visit your folks—you can guess the rest.'

Chapter Eighteen

Although Tim had only recently returned from a short but well-earned break with his parents following the last strenuous criminal investigation, Ann generously covered the cost for his next visit.

He had told his folks he would take an Uber taxi from Coolangatta Airport on the Gold Coast and found them at home waiting to welcome him.

His mother's home-cooked meal was welcoming. Being a bachelor had its disadvantages when it came to preparing food and eating alone, although Ann often indulged him.

After he caught up with both his parents that evening, Tim took out his laptop and gathered the information he needed about Edwina Thorpe—ready to commence tracking her the following day. He would start with an address he had noted at No.2, Branwell Lane, Florence, near Dreamworld and quite a distance from his parents' home—at least half an hour's drive.

There was a knock at his bedroom door.

'Tim, it's Mum—Dad asked if you're coming into the lounge for a nightcap before turning in?'

He jumped off his desk in the room and came to the door. 'Yeah, sure. Tell him I'll be there in ten.'

Tim was glad his father elected to spend time with him, as while he and his sister Bonny were growing up, they frequently missed out on having much contact—he was always too preoccupied with his business ventures.

His father poured two glasses of Port while his mother walked in with a glass of wine.

'So, Dad. Have you had any snake bites lately?' Tim teased.

'Snakes—I wouldn't mock it too much. Our neighbour had one crawl out of a large pot plant last week.'

'Dinkum? I was just pulling your leg. You told me on my previous visit that a few snakes had come down the river during a storm and were found on neighbouring properties.'

'Nothing unusual around here. We had them in Sydney too, you know.'

'I don't understand why you want to stay over here. We have nothing like that in New Zealand, and Queensland is full of creepie-crawlies.'

'It's a bit late for us to go back to NZ now, Tim. While you and your sister were still at school, we stayed put, but it was a dream we always had—to live in Queensland. Now we're about to retire, we can fulfil our aspirations.'

'Yeah, but in a place with poisonous snakes and deadly spiders.'

'It's not as bad as you think. There's a lovely golf club here and we've made lots of friends. The coast is beautiful.'

Tim gave up thinking his parents would ever return to their homeland. It was time he started building a new life for himself—which he would have done if his fiancée, Mary, were still alive. His sister, Bonny, was married and living in America, but she and her husband were heavily occupied with their jobs. This meant that Tim seldom saw his sister, except sometimes at Christmas. Perhaps he needed to get out and meet girls—that's if his Aunty Ann would give him sufficient time off. But he would have to let go of Mary first—or he'd never be able to move on.

'Are you still with us, Tim?' His mother's voice rattled him back to reality.

'Sorry, Mum. I've got an interesting case on right now and have to get off to work early in the morning. I told you over the phone I need to track this witness who lives on the other side of the city. Can I borrow your car—or perhaps I can hire one for a few days?'

'Of course. I don't need it tomorrow—I've taken a few days off while you're here.'

***

Meg's lawyer, Sheldon, had been on the ball. From the documents she'd handed him earlier in the week, he'd discovered that Lyle had hidden their relational assets and had emptied their personal and business bank accounts—siphoning off their joint property.

Leaning forward in the soft leather armchair next to Sheldon's office desk, Meg was eager to tell him all she knew that could shed a light on Lyle's covert activity.

'This husband of yours has certainly been a busy boy—wife-beater, adulterer, and now he appears to be a fraudster.'

'Yes, he's all of that. Have you been through the bank statements already?'

'No, I haven't—but Sydney, my accountant, has gone through them with a fine-toothed comb. I see what you mean—he has left you

123

nothing. You still have savings in your own account though.'

Meg's skin turned the translucent colour it usually did when she was stressed.

'What? The piddly few hundred dollars I have left to feed myself. I already owe my sister a lot of money. Without her, I wouldn't have survived this ordeal.'

'Yes, you're right. I can see from that bank statement you showed me where you had received the large inheritance from your parents' estate. Afterwards it was transferred to an account in your husband's name—do you know why that happened—did you consent to it?'

Meg's cheeks flushed with embarrassment. 'I guess I was pretty naïve way back then. When he purchased our marital home, he said he would invest the rest of the money for our future at a high interest.'

'Yes, I see the deeds of your property are in Lyle's name only. I thought perhaps that was his house prior to you getting engaged—crafty sod. But I can't see where the rest of the funds have been deposited. It appears it could be in an offshore account.'

Meg's face dropped. 'Oh, no. Does that mean I won't be able to retrieve them?'

'We don't know that for sure. Tim, your associate, could help you with that. I believe he is a cyber fraud expert and will have experience in tracing hidden bank accounts. He'll be much cheaper than using my Forensic Accountant.'

Meg appeared perplexed. 'So ... can't you do anything else to help me right now?' Her voice quavered.

'Oh, yes, of course there's a lot I can do. First of all, I need to get an order from the court for the discovery of assets and Lyle will be requested to disclose all your matrimonial property. He won't get away with hiding it for much longer.'

Sheldon went on to explain that he'd already applied for legal aid to assist her with litigation expenses until the court was able to free up her assets.

Meg knew she would manage with the financial assistance she was already receiving from her local Work and Income agency to tide her over. Now her life was changing—she was beginning to feel empowered. Although the butterfly's wings were crumpled, she was about to fly.

Chapter Nineteen

Tim had been going around in circles since early morning on the first day of his search for Eddie on the Gold Coast. After looking her up on the electoral roll and discovering her last listed address in Florence, he had got nowhere. There were new tenants in the townhouse, and none of them knew who she was. So he continued to search the web and discovered that Eddie had a site advertising Events Management.

'Darn!' He sat in his car and rested his head on the steering wheel. Pulling himself together, he picked up his iPhone and jumped onto Facebook. That was one place he had already searched, but Eddie's account was private, and there was no profile photo for him to compare.

'I know—I'll send a message to say I have critical news about an old friend of hers. I'll see if she can meet me in town,' he muttered to himself.

He drove down by the waterfront and eventually found a carpark. It was time for lunch, and he was famished after all the driving around in heavy traffic. He ambled along the boulevard to one of his favourite beachside cafes and ordered a full breakfast, seeing that all he had eaten since early that morning was an apple.

He sat drinking his large flat white, watching a few seagulls scavenging the remnants of someone's cast-off fries strewn on the edge of the wharf.

What was he going to do now? He'd exhausted most avenues at trying to track down this elusive woman. He and Ann had decided she would be able to provide them with many answers to help them with their investigation, and now all hope of that happening was beginning to fade.

Tim sat with his face resting on clasped hands, leaning his elbows on the café table.

'Is everything alright, sir—can I get you anything else—another coffee, or perhaps a beer?'

The young waitress must have discerned his downcast demeanour and had decided to check him out. Embarrassed, he regained his composure.

'No, everything's fine thanks—lovely meal. I'll just have my bill now.'

Tim got up and followed the girl to the counter where he paid for his meal and then wandered out onto the boulevard. Just as he stood deciding where to go next, his phone dinged. He stopped to check his Facebook messages. To his delight he'd received one from Eddie. Taking a seat on a wooden bench at the edge of the sidewalk, his heart pounded as he read the content.

The woman had replied to his message, and after a few more chats back and forth, she agreed to meet late that afternoon at another café of her choice called the Lighthouse.

The weather had changed. Outside, the temperature had risen to 30 degrees Celsius since Tim had left the house. Now he was cooking, as he was not used to living with such extremes of heat.

He wanted to spend the rest of the afternoon cooling off and couldn't wait to change out of his long-sleeved white shirt. A swim at the wonderful manmade beach pool at Streets Beach South Bank before meeting Eddie would be a great idea. But first he had to head back home to collect his swimming gear.

Tim felt bad about being out all day after his mother had taken time off for him. Before setting off, he promised he would shout her and his father a meal at the restaurant he knew they enjoyed visiting.

'Can you ring and book a table for tomorrow evening please, Mum?' He also hoped he might have some good news when he phoned Ann later.

At the pool, refreshed from his swim, Tim checked his appearance again before he left the change room. He hoped the walk back to the carpark to throw his bathing gear into his vehicle would dry his thick mop.

After securing his vehicle, he took another look at himself in the passenger window, combing his fingers through his hair and swishing the loose strands back in place. He tucked his white short-sleeved shirt back into his camel-coloured cotton chinos and checked the name of the café he had noted on his phone before picking up his briefcase.

Chapter Twenty

Ah—the Lighthouse. There it is. Tim hoped he would be able to recognise Eddie, who said she would be wearing a red top. In no time at all, as he approached the café front, he spotted the woman sitting with a glass of water, biting her nails. Eddie's rosy cheeks blended in well with her blood-red blouse contrasting her flaxen hair. She appeared to be around his age.

Eddie's face flushed as Tim approached her, appearing agitated. Her eyes darted around nervously, as if to make sure there were witnesses for whatever might take place. She settled once Tim spoke.

'Eddie, is it? My name's Tim Martin.' He passed her his business card. 'Mind if I sit down?'

'No, please do. I'm eager to find out what you want with me.' Her voice shook. 'Am I in trouble?'

Tim flashed his investigator's licence. He guessed it could be unnerving being handed an ID from a strange private investigator. He leaned his briefcase against the leg of the dining table.

She jumped in before he could answer. 'Am I being investigated?'

'It's a long story. We're not after you exactly—it's another person who's under scrutiny, and we're hoping you can help us.'

Eddie's eyes stayed focused on his business card. 'Mmm, Ann Grieves—I remember reading about her. She was the one who covered the case with that dodgy Softsculpt factory in Auckland. They were a bunch of fraudsters, I read, and several of them were tried and imprisoned in Britain. I followed that inquiry—it was captivating.'

'I'm Ann Grieves's business partner. We solved that case together, and it was a hefty one at that.'

Tim realised it was rather prideful to put himself forward, but he'd placed his life on the line trying to apprehend that Softsculpt bunch of criminals and had certainly earned his wages.

Eddie flipped through the beverage list and then handed it to Tim. He glanced through it and waved at the waiter. 'I'll get this—what would you like?'

Eddie gave him a stop sign with her hand. 'If you don't mind, I'll get my own. We've only just met.' Tim cringed at her assertiveness and sat back.

The waiter took their drink orders and refilled their water glasses. Making sure the fellow was not within hearing distance, Tim began to question Eddie.

'We have concluded that you are Edwina Thorpe, known as Eddie. What would you like me to call you?'

'Eddie is fine. I use my full name Edwina for business, mostly.'

'And you were born and raised in New Zealand—right?'

'Yes, that's correct—but I've spent the last ten years here in Australia since I started my career as an Events Manager after graduating from university in Auckland.'

'We have evidence that you had contracts with a drone company called *High Flyers*. Is that true?'

'That's right. They were the first events I managed when I set up my own business, and I was highly successful too.'

Tim had uncharitable thoughts about how she was able to achieve such success with that company, being so young, and then he kept his judgemental thoughts to himself.

'Was that straight after you graduated from university?'

'No—I was employed by another corporate organisation in Sydney first, and then when I went out on my own, I set up my business here.'

A waiter brought Tim his beer and a glass of white wine for Eddie before taking their meal orders. They both chose the stuffed chicken breast and Greek salad with sourdough. By the time their food had arrived, they'd broken the ice with small talk, then their conversation became more serious.

'You've come a long way to talk to me,' said Eddie.

'I'm staying with my parents just out of town and have come to see if you can help with our enquiries. We're investigating a man called Lyle Doyle from Auckland and have discovered correspondence that shows you've had a close connection with him—in fact, you were his lover several years ago.'

Eddie almost choked on her food and picked up her glass of wine, taking a large mouthful. 'Humph! Is that what he told you—a liar right to the end?'

'Oh, so it's not true then?' Tim waited before he mentioned the love letters and cards.

'You're right about being lovers. That was a long time ago, before we were married. Then the romance all stopped, and the abuse began.'

Tim, too, almost choked on the sourdough bread he had just put into his mouth.

'Married—when was that? We never knew he was divorced and thought his current wife in Auckland was his first.'

Eddie stopped eating and put down her utensils. She took another gulp of wine. 'I'm still his wife, although I would rather believe he was dead—what are you talking about?'

Tim was puzzled. He wondered if she was telling the truth and shook his head and grimaced.

'You aren't wearing a wedding ring. How do I know this is true?'

'I can prove it to you—I'll show you my marriage certificate. I was always going to apply for a divorce when Lyle left to go overseas somewhere. Initially, I tried to locate him via his drone company called *High Flyers* in Brisbane and Auckland, but he'd sold the factories and the manufacturer has renamed their business, *Air Tech*. The new owners told me they couldn't give me Lyle's contact details but said they would pass on my messages for him to call me—he never did.'

Tim's eyebrows crinkled. It was difficult for him to follow her conversation. 'So, what about the divorce?'

'Eventually I gave up on pursuing it. I was relieved to be well shod of him and had decided I would never marry again, anyway. Out of sight—out of mind.'

For the next hour and a few more glasses of wine together, including a rich dessert, the two continued to swap notes. It was as mind-boggling for Tim as it was for Eddie—the revelation that Lyle was a true-blue bigamist, serial abuser and added to the bargain, a compulsive liar.

Chapter Twenty-one

Tim felt an overwhelming compassion for Eddie who was too young to have endured such heartache and damage. He sat listening with intent to Eddie's story—how Lyle had lured her into his dark web while she was working as a freelance events manager on several contracts with his company, *High Flyers*.

He wasn't keen on marriage for a few years while they courted but married her when he discovered her father was a considerably wealthy businessman with his own advertising company. They moved into Eddie's bungalow, and a week after they married the abuse began. It was verbal, psychological, emotional and even physical battering, which she described in detail to Tim.

Lyle had badgered and belittled his wife to such a degree, that he drove her out of her home, which she had already owned.

Tim's eyes narrowed. 'Why do you think he wanted rid of you so much? He could still have done his gallivanting while still living with you.'

'I had been told by specialist doctors I would never be able to bear a child after they discovered I was born with a retroverted womb, so we didn't take any precautions—but they were wrong. Several months after we married, I was expecting Lyle's baby.'

Tim leaned in closer. 'What? He should have been delighted about that ... what happened, if you don't mind me asking ... about the baby?'

'I don't mind. I gave birth to a healthy girl by Caesarean Section. Lyle wouldn't believe the baby was his and insisted I'd been playing around, but that was untrue—I was always a one-man girl. He became increasingly resentful, as though we were raising another man's child, even though Sophie looked just like him!' Her voice began to crack.

With a face full of sorrow, Tim observed multiple crow's feet surrounding her eyes— telltale signs of years of emotional turmoil in a time past.

Tim had asked if Eddie would allow him to take notes, which she had agreed, but he found it difficult keeping up, let alone reading his own writing. He would have to get her to write out a full witness statement before he left Brisbane.

Once Eddie had relaxed with a few glasses of wine under her belt, Tim began to gain her trust, and she couldn't stop once she had started expounding on the vile exploits of her husband Lyle Doyle.

She told how he'd treated her in the same way he'd abused Meg. It appeared he did it in such a way to force his wives to leave by intimidating them so that they would never return. He would quickly work his evil way at extorting whatever money he could from their joint bank accounts. Eddie had been shrewd enough not to allow him to operate all their finances in his name. She was sharp in business but, like Meg, naïve in relationships.

'Coffee, Eddie? I'm going to get one.' Tim called the waiter over. She agreed, and he gave the order to the young man waiting on their table.

'Tell me about your daughter, Sophie, if that's okay. Is she with you?'

'Absolutely. My younger sister lives near me, and she helped with nannying for years after

Lyle forced me out and still supports me a great deal.'

'What did you do when he drove you out of your own home—where did you go?'

'Dad came to my rescue and threatened to publish an article in the main newspaper warning innocent young women that they may become his next victim. Lyle promptly gave me the house back and within days had packed up and left to go abroad—God knows where. He's a Kiwi and had worked and lived in Brisbane travelling back and forth from Auckland while setting up the processing plant for manufacturing his drones.'

Tim almost lifted a hand to comfort her but pulled back. He knew not to get involved with his witnesses in that way. 'But you were married in Brisbane?'

'Yes, we lived together for two years after we married until it all broke down. Before that, we only saw each other when he came over on business trips and for the rest of the time wrote letters and chatted online. I'm certain there were other women too that he met on the internet.'

'What about Sophie's birth certificate?'

Eddie set her jaw. 'What do you mean?' she began tugging on her fingers nervously.

'Sorry, I need to ask if Lyle's name is on it?'

'No, he wouldn't let me use it. I had to put my maiden name on the form. When Sophie is old enough, she can change it if she chooses. I'll tell her the truth about her father one day.'

'Are you still a freelance events manager?'

'Not any more. I had intended taking my business to New Zealand, but after that fiasco, I completely lost my confidence and gave it up. I only work as a casual employee on wages part-time in Brisbane now. Anyway, I wouldn't return to Auckland with that mongrel alive and well living there.'

'So, he doesn't pay child maintenance of any kind?'

'No way—he has evaded that one.'

Tim explained that with the string of criminal convictions lining up, he was going to end up behind bars.

'I'm going to have to head back to Auckland in a few days. I would greatly appreciate if you could write out your story involving your marriage to Lyle, and I'll collect it from you before I leave. If you could sign it, that would be an immense help. I'll be in touch.'

They finished their drinks. 'Please let me get this bill. Perhaps you can shout me another time if we meet up again.'

Eddie nodded her approval, then Tim paid at the counter while she stood aside.

When he walked his priceless witness to her car, he felt a burden for the woman who appeared like a bird that had been crushed in a heavy hand. He was tempted to give her a hug but refrained, aware that with her vulnerability she may form an attachment to him. And he just wasn't ready for a new relationship.

Tim spent the next day paying attention to his mother, and in the evening he took both his parents out for dinner as promised.

The day before returning to Auckland, he received a phone call from Eddie who asked him to drop by and collect her signed witness statement. He was excited to see her. She handed him certified copies of her marriage certificate and Sophie's birth records, which saved him from applying to the authorities for them. She also included various wedding pictures of her marriage to Lyle, as well as a clear photo of him holding Sophie as a baby. This was exactly what Tim and Ann needed to make an initial conviction.

Chapter Twenty-two

Ann waited eagerly at Auckland Airport for Tim to walk through the Arrivals area, scanning the long line of passengers who had already disembarked. The flight could not have been full, as she spotted Tim quickly and rushed up to greet him. Despite refraining from hugging him in public, she'd missed him a great deal.

'I'm sure you've packed on a few kilos.' Ann helped him load his luggage onto the back seat of the Land Rover. 'Must be your Mum's home cooking.'

'I didn't get to eat much during my time there, unfortunately—I was hardly at home. But I've got some pivotal results that will interest you.'

During the trip back from the airport, Tim gave Ann a report of all he had learned about Eddie. Finally she had some evidence for a case against Lyle, as they'd been going around in circles only producing circumstantial evidence. Even if he had been a serial adulterer, that wasn't solid enough to put him behind bars. If Meg could produce medical reports and X-Rays that proved the injuries Lyle gave her—especially the head injury leaving her with permanent damage—that would weigh pretty heavily in court, although may not land him in jail.

But both these detectives were now on a proper winning streak—one that was not so common but carried a maximum penalty—bigamy.

'I think your success in Brisbane deserves a celebration, partner. I'm going to take you to that little restaurant near my house where I shouted dinner the last time.'

'You don't have to do that. It was all part of my job and I had to visit my folks, anyway.'

'Stop being so modest, Tim, and just accept it. I'll book a table for seven.'

'I just remembered—how did you get on with that tracking app I put on your phone to trace the movements of Lyle's vehicle? Has he been a naughty boy again?'

'It stopped suddenly. He was just making a few trips back and forth to Clovelly Beach and then there was nothing. When I turn the app on, the screen turns black.'

'Ah-ha, that's not good.'

'What do you mean—is my phone dying?'

'No, it means that Lyle is on to us and has removed the app. He has most likely taken the Ute to a mechanic for a Warrant check, and they would have pointed the tracking device out to him. He has removed it, which means he knows someone is trailing him.'

Ann pressed her hands on her hips. 'Well, shrewd as he is, we can still be one step ahead of him. I can obtain the authority to check the passenger lists at the airport to see if he's in the country, as he may have vanished already. I'll get an alert placed on him.'

***

After Ann had dropped Tim off at home, she called into the Cockle Cove Police Station to see Bryce Drummond who'd asked her to update him on the Meg Doyle case, as he would soon be getting involved. While Tim was away, Meg had given Ann her consent to bring Bryce, the local Detective Inspector, in on her investigation whenever necessary. Ann seldom wanted to let go of her private clients and get the police involved unless the state of play turned violent or there was a murder or organised crime to solve.

'Bigamy! It has been many years since I've dealt with anything like that.' Bryce pulled out a chair for Ann. 'Plonk yourself down here and I'll ask one of my constables to grab us a couple of coffees.'

While he wandered off down the corridor, Ann pulled out the copies of Eddie's marriage certificate and Sophie's birth records along with the photos which Tim had given her. A few minutes later, a young constable brought in the Flat Whites and placed them on the DI's office desk and left the room.

When Bryce returned, Ann elaborated on the information Tim had shared with her on the way back from the airport.

The DI perused the documents on his desk.

'I wouldn't go in all guns blazing and arrest Doyle just yet. Perhaps you and Tim need to find out what you can about this new woman he is seeing in Clovelly Beach. If he has abused two women already, it's likely he'll be doing the same to this one. It'll be tricky, as you won't want him to get wind of it—or he'll scarper like a bat out of hell. Patty needs to know he already has two wives if he has given her expectations of marrying her anytime soon.'

'That's what I was thinking. I'll need some help with interviewing him about the wife battering if you don't mind—at the station. We would need to be close to an arrest about the bigamy, first. I'm going to talk to Meg tomorrow and let her know her husband is a bigamist, which makes her marriage null and void.'

'Lucky girl—she won't have to go through divorce proceedings now but can still claim half of her relationship property to which she is legally entitled.' Bryce stood up and patted her on the shoulder. 'Well done, Calamity—you're a star.'

'No, don't give the credit to me—it's Tim you should congratulate. He did most of the digging, both in the forest behind Meg's house and in the dirt he found on the web.' She replied with a wry smile.

'I already said he should be working here at Cockle Cove Station. You nabbed him before I did, so I guess he belongs to you.' Bryce gave her a playful wink. 'Let me know how you get on with young Meg tomorrow and whether she is prepared to testify against Doyle in court when he goes to trial.'

'It's a mighty breakthrough for her now that she can be released from him through his criminal offense of bigamy. She was beginning to think nobody would believe her in court if she told them about his battering and psychological abuse. Most of it was invisible to others.'

'You're right, Calamity Ann. Remember, you told me once that your Vicar friend, Thomas, said that those things that are done in the darkness lose their power when brought out into the light.'

'So, you remembered. I've found it to be true in cases like Meg's. People who've been covert psychological hostages of abusers, regain their confidence when their perpetrator's atrocities have been exposed.'

'You're correct about her being kept like a butterfly in a jar. I think you'll find now that this creature will undergo a metamorphosis and take flight,' he said, with smiling eyes.

Ann loved listening to Bryce's sensitive and intuitive insights. If she were keen to remarry, he would be the kind of man who would interest her. But she quickly banished that idea, as it would interfere with their working relationship and strong friendship.

'Are you still with me, Ann? I'm afraid I'm going to have to move—I've got a few interviews to conduct shortly. Get back to me tomorrow.'

She was embarrassed and hoped he couldn't read her thoughts. 'Of course, I must get a move on too.' She turned and hurried down the corridor, still feeling the warm flush in her cheeks.

Chapter Twenty-three

Scout looked longingly at Ann, hoping she would take him in the car to one of his favourite beaches where dogs were permitted to run unleashed. Often she would allow him to ride with her when making brief visits to witnesses and afterwards take him for a long run along the beach. He was her constant companion when Tim wasn't around.

'Hold on, Scout—let me make a few more copies of these papers, and then we'll be off.'

After printing the documents, she grabbed the dog's leash from its hook and headed out to Woodlands to talk to Meg. On the way, she drove down to Cornwall Bay and let Scout out for a good run. Panting, she struggled to catch up. As the dog had a fetish for trying to eat dead fish washed up on the beach, she didn't take her eyes off him.

Ann realised how far removed she was from her days in the police force when she'd received awards for endurance and bravery. One incident she recalled well was the day she sprinted a great distance across a field, jumping into a river to rescue a woman and child in a sinking car. Those were the days when she was at her fittest—a far cry from the person she was now.

'Come back here, Scout. Heel!' Ann's reminiscing made her take her eye off the ball and was just in time to catch the dog about to roll in the remnants of a dead seagull.

'That's enough—back to the car.'

***

Meg was home alone this time. Pete was at work, and Angela had popped out to the village on some errands. Ann could see that Meg was regaining her confidence with the assistance of a sound lawyer and several sessions of counselling under her belt that Angela had organised for her.

Meg sat Ann down at the dining table after asking if she would join her in a cup of freshly made expresso coffee. She ducked into the kitchen and returned to sit at the table with her visitor.

'I've got good news for once. Sheldon, my lawyer, has threatened to take Lyle to court if he doesn't pay me for half the house as he'd promised. He also told Lyle's lawyer that I'll get two independent valuations of both the house and the business.'

'Oh, that's good—I take my hat off to him. He's really on the job not letting him get away with anything.'

'Sheldon's great. I feel he's on my side and wants justice for me.'

'Well, honey—that's what you're paying him for ... now ... I have a heap of interesting news for you too.'

Meg poured the coffee she'd prepared in Angela's new expresso machine.

Ann grinned. 'I wondered what all the hissing and roaring was about in the kitchen.'

She handed Ann a plate with her sister's home baking.

'Mmm, peanut brownies. I'm sorry to decline, but I'm working on the battle of the bulge right now.'

Her hostess chuckled and put the plate out of reach. 'So, what's the news?'

'You may want to finish eating and try not to choke on your biscuit.'

Meg's face puckered.

'Oh, it's not bad news—at least I don't think so,' said Ann. 'It'll be a shocking relief for you, I think.'

Ann carefully constructed her sentences to buffer the blow when Meg was about to find out that her marriage had been a complete sham and was now null and void. At first, she hesitated, wondering if it would be best for Angela to be there to support her sister when she dropped the bombshell but changed her mind. Meg had been kept in the dark for long enough, and Lyle needed to be completely exposed.

'Is everything alright, Ann—what's happened now?'

The detective expounded on how Tim visited the woman, Eddie, in Brisbane and the outcome of that interview.

'Here are photocopies of Eddie's marriage certificate—and photos relating to that relationship and their daughter. You can keep these, as they'll help you grasp the truth. I understand it's going to be difficult to get your head around it all.'

'What—Lyle has a child to another woman?'

Meg gaped at the documents and photographs with her mouth open, frozen to her seat, not knowing whether to smile or cry. She did shed tears, but for joy, not dismay.

'Thank you, Ann, for bringing me this revelation. As you say—I'm so relieved that finally they'll believe me in court.'

Meg threw her arms around her. 'I knew Lyle was hiding something pretty sinister. He resented me but needed my finances. That poor girl—and what about this new one Tim saw him kissing that night—are you going to warn her?'

'We don't want to frighten Lyle off until we have all our evidence and can make an arrest. We have to gather together the documents to present in court. Eddie has signed a witness statement and now I'll need an official one from you unless you're prepared to stand up in court to testify.'

Meg's forehead wrinkled as she looked at her gold wedding ring, rolling it on her finger and then suddenly yanking at it hard until it slid off.

'This is going in the bin!' She clutched the ring in a tight fist.

'Can I think about it or talk to Angela and Pete first? I'm not sure I can stand up in a courtroom with Lyle glaring at me. I know how those defence lawyers work—they'll tear me apart, and I doubt my nerves could take it.'

Ann tensed—afraid that she was going to back out. Meg was a key witness along with Eddie, who'd told Tim she would fly to Auckland and face Lyle in court if necessary.

But two cords were stronger than one, Ann decided. If she and Tim could convince both aggrieved wives to attend Lyle's trial, they had a better chance of putting the rogue behind bars, at least for a short time, to teach him a lesson so that he wouldn't wreck another woman's life.

Ann heard a vehicle's tyres crunching outside on the gravel driveway and craned her neck to see that Angela had arrived. *Just in the nick of time*, she thought.

While Angela stood transfixed, holding a bag full of groceries, Ann proceeded to break the news about Lyle's bigamy. The woman looked bug-eyed at her and then caught herself— realising that her sister needed comforting. She offloaded her shopping and went to her side.

Ann left Angela to console Meg, who waved Eddie's marriage certificate, Sophie's birth records, and the photos under her nose.

As she left the house, Ann quietly rejoiced that Meg's persecutor was about to be caught.

There was still time for her to visit the Leisure Centre to do a few lengths of the swimming pool. If she didn't exercise on a regular basis, Ann knew she would get stiff from driving or sitting around. Her recovery program as a seasoned *foodie* had to come first in her life. When she was in the police force as a Detective Inspector, sprinting a hundred metres was a small feat for Ann. But these days, she doubted she could last the distance chasing a criminal. That's why she'd got Tim onboard.

Chapter Twenty-four

After the startling news both she and Angela had received, Meg suddenly pulled herself together, and her demeanour took on a different tone. She was enraged that she'd foolishly endured Lyle's shocking abuse all those years. Unbeknown to her, their marriage had been a farce—null and void. That struck an even crueller blow than the verbal and physical treatment put together.

'He'll pay for this,' Meg snapped, as Angela looked on, taken aback at her sister's sudden change in character. It wasn't Meg's nature to be harsh or aggressive, and Angela tried to pacify her.

'Let me make you a cup of chamomile tea to settle your nerves—you've had a nasty shock.'

'I'm going out, Angela—please don't fuss, I'll be okay. I need to go for a drive in the car and assimilate the barrage of information Ann gave me.'

Angela awkwardly withdrew her arm from around Meg's shoulder. 'Well, please be careful—you've had quite an upset, and your nerves aren't too good right now.'

'I know—it's more than just an upset. But from now on, I'm going to be perfectly fine. I feel I'm getting my power back and neither Lyle nor any other man will ever crush me again!'

Angela went quiet, observing the strong set in her sister's jaw—an obvious expression of defiance. At times like this, it was best to let her go. She was on a mission, and no one was going to stop her, Angela realised.

Meg excused herself to and went to her bedroom to check the details of Patty's address. She'd stored it in her handbag after obtaining the information from Tim. Furtively stepping into Pete's office, she printed copies of the documents and photos that Ann had given her. For the first time in years, she was thinking logically, and planning moves to extricate the other woman from the web that her mendacious husband had woven.

***

Lyle had usually driven their Peugeot and had made sure it possessed all the modern gadgets, so Meg was grateful for the GPS. It made it so much easier to find her way as she sped along the tortuous coastal road.

Discovering her husband's double life—after the initial shock—seemed to empower her. At least he would be found guilty of a criminal offense, and hopefully that would be sufficient to stop him from harassing her.

Her mind was severely distracted as she suddenly swerved at a cat that almost shot under her front car wheels, causing her to pull over onto the shoulder of the road.

'Whew! That was close,' she uttered, peering through her window in the gap between the Pohutukawa trees on the sheer cliffs across the road. She guessed the drop would be at least a hundred metres to the beach below, maybe more.

She shuddered and pulled herself together, reiterating self-talk about being a strong woman—a tool she'd received from her therapy sessions. Meg had a strong faith in God once, but that had been knocked out of her after years of Lyle's battering. Perhaps she could regain that trust in her maker once all this was over—but for now, she was stuck in survival mode.

Making sure she was mentally intact before setting off down the road, she drew a deep breath and let it out slowly. After taking a brief look at the map on the vehicle's GPS, Patty's address in Clovelly Road suddenly came into view.

Driving towards the residential area in Clovelly Heights, Meg could tell by the palatial white homes that this was an affluent area. Her eyes were on stalks as she drove up a few streets that led to Patty's house and gaped in awe at the sight of a massive Queenslander home before her. *Mmm, someone must be sitting on a goldmine.* She wondered if this Patty woman might hold some kind of political office to be able to afford such an estate.

She pulled up outside and checked herself in the car mirror—taking a comb from the glove box and tidying up her fringe.

Meg sat quietly, inhaling the salty sea air, then pulled her shoulders back, pushed her chest out and told herself she'd nothing to fear. She was ready for action and excited about any information she could get out of Patty—but more so—would she reveal other skeletons in the closet that Lyle may still be hiding? She reached for her document satchel on the back seat. It was now or never.

Chapter Twenty-five

Meg strode boldly up the red brick pathway lined with white roses, hoping and praying Patty would be home.

Usually her knock would be feeble, but this time she pounded at the door. A net curtain at the window moved aside as a face appeared.

Meg was shocked. The girl appeared to be only in her twenties. 'Cradle-snatcher,' she muttered quietly, before anyone answered the door.

'Hello—what can I do for you?' The girl smiled sweetly, glancing down at the satchel in Meg's held in her hand—resembling an insurance salesperson.

'I ... my name is Meg, and I desperately need to talk to you about something personal. I'm not a salesperson and I'm trying to protect you, Patty.'

The girl's face changed as she hesitated, obviously not knowing whether to trust Meg.

'How do you know my name?'

'Would you mind if I come in, please? You'll thank me for this—I guarantee it.'

Patty led her through a side gate to the back of the massive home, where they sat down at a table surrounded by an engaging flower garden. Meg wondered why she hadn't invited her inside the house.

Patty was blunt. 'We can sit out here and talk—what is it?'

Meg opened her document satchel containing copies of hers and Eddie's marriage certificate, which Ann had given her along with their corresponding wedding photos. Amongst these was also a copy of Sophie's birth record—although Lyle was not named as father—and snapshots of her. Meg wasted no time in first showing the unsuspecting victim the wedding photos of Lyle and herself, and then pictures of him getting married to Eddie.

Patty's eyes flashed. 'What's going on—is this a joke?' She stared closer at the snapshots and threw them on the table as Meg was distracted by a silver ring glittering with diamonds the size of a plum. *That must be her engagement ring,* she guessed.

'Is that you in these wedding photos with Lyle? And is this other woman getting married to him too? I don't understand.'

Meg rattled off as fast as she could the hideous truth about the scoundrel who had taken this poor girl hostage. By the time she'd finished expounding on the history of her tempestuous marriage to Lyle and given Patty all she knew about Eddie's experience, the girl caved in and began to snivel. Between large sobs, she opened up.

Meg slipped her hand back into the satchel and took out a photo of Lyle holding baby Sophie, passing it to Patty. 'It gets worse, sorry— he had a child to Eddie too.'

Patty held a hand in front of her mouth. 'The toerag! How could he keep all this hidden for so many years?'

Meg held up another photo of Sophie as a young girl who had a close likeness to her father in facial features.

'And he told me he didn't want any children! Made me stay childless all those years,' Meg whined. 'See what pain you have fortunately avoided? He only wants women like us for our money and selfish ambition.'

'It's obvious he's a gold digger. My father is Michael Gregg, the top Foreign Correspondent who owns the newspaper Worldglobe. I'm the senior editor and write a column for him. As soon as Lyle found that out, he proposed—but before he knew about my dad owning the newspaper, he was indifferent about making a commitment to me.'

Meg scanned the devastation in the girl's face and touched her arm, then retracted it—not wanting to appear over-familiar.

'I'm so sorry to drop this on you, Patty. But perhaps we can help each other through it. The crime investigator heading the case, Ann Grieves, needs all the evidence she can get to put him behind bars.'

Patty shrugged. 'Well, where do we go from here? Lyle is due back sometime soon, but he hasn't let me know the date of his arrival yet. He loves to keep me in the dark, and only God knows where he gets to on his trips.'

'Look—the police now have sufficient evidence to arrest him on bigamy charges. Perhaps you could tell them about your relationship with him. Did he abuse you too?'

Tears rolled down Patty's face as she detailed the inconsistencies in Lyle's behaviour during their short relationship, although she had agreed to marry him.

'He's controlling with me too, even while overseas—phoning me on video every five minutes, demanding I report to him my every move. He even has cameras in the house which he had installed after we became engaged. That's why I didn't invite you inside. But I can go and make us a drink if you like.'

'Oh, no thanks. I'd rather get this sorted out and then I have some business to do before I go home.'

'Let's go for a walk along the clifftop. There are several beautiful gardens and homes along the walkway, and we can talk some more.'

Meg was desperate to extract more history from Patty. 'Okay, great idea. I'll just grab my walking shoes from the car.'

'Oh, you won't need those. The walkway is a well-trodden track in the middle of a Reserve of private manicured lawns that are easy underfoot.'

The girls wandered through the gap in the neatly clipped knee-high Box hedge out onto the path that led alongside elegant clifftop homes. Some of the houses were secured with high hedges or fences, probably to prevent young children from plummeting down the cliffs. Others had no barrier at all, apart from a garden bed of flowers or vegetables. In some places, there was just a sheer drop to the beach below.

Patty searched her guest's face. 'Was Lyle violent with you at any time?'

Meg quickly elaborated on the types of battering she'd received from Lyle and then directed her attention on Patty—eager to find more dirt for the detectives.

'How about you?'

Patty's face fell. There was a moment of silence before she answered.

'He lost his temper several times and pushed me on more than one occasion. But the worst was his psychological control, and lately I've begun to have doubts about getting married. You've come in the nick of time,' she whimpered.

The girls continued to share their experiences of living with a narcissist until they turned and walked back to the house.

'I'd best get going now.' Meg stopped for a moment to take in the panoramic view.

'I can leave the papers and photos with you, as I have more copies at home, and I'll come and see you again soon.'

'I'd love you to visit again another day—although—there's a chance you might run into Lyle when you visit next.'

Meg shook her head 'Well, I don't think that's likely. He's going to face the music soon, as Ann Grieves says he'll be arrested at the airport when he arrives back in the country.'

'I hope so, but I'm going to put an end to our relationship when he gets back.'

'I'd best get going now. Please promise not to tell Lyle I was here if he contacts you.'

'Of course, I won't. Thank you so much, Meg. I know you have put your neck out coming here like this and we sisters must stick together. Pity Eddie can't join us. Maybe we should invite her to come over if Lyle is arrested.'

'Good thinking. Let's talk about it next time we get together.' Before Meg picked up her document satchel and headed for the side gate accompanied by Patty, they swapped phone numbers.

Chapter Twenty-six

Ann came off the phone from talking to Bryce with a broad smile plastered over her face.

'It's going to happen, Tim! Lyle was on a flight to Switzerland last week, and Bryce finally has sufficient evidence to arrest him. The airport police will do that when he arrives here, but his lawyer wouldn't give me the exact date and is mucking us about.'

'Are you sure we can't contact Patty and let her know what he is really like?'

'No—if we do that, she could alert him, and then he'll most likely hide out in Europe somewhere.'

Tim gave her a wry smile as he pulled on his motorcycle helmet and walked to the door. 'Maybe Patty will be happy to get rid of him.'

Ann rattled her car keys. 'Bryce wants us at the station in the morning to review what to do next once Lyle is back in the country. I'll see you there at nine. Thanks for dropping off that information I wanted. I'll talk to you in the morning.'

As Ann listened to the fading sound of Tim's Ducati flying down the driveway and out onto the road, her phone rang again. Checking her caller ID, she could see that it was Meg, just the person she wanted to speak to.

Meg rattled off a barrage of news about Lyle's engagement to Patty and how he had treated her. Ann almost dropped the phone with much consternation.

She tried to contain her anger, knowing how fragile Meg was still. 'What! We asked you not to go there yet. We are waiting to arrest him at the airport and don't want you to frighten him off, or he'll scarper, for sure.'

'Patty won't warn him and told me she'll help see him behind bars.'

'I know you're in a great deal of pain, Meg, and have every reason to want to confront him. But please—not yet. You'll get your chance in court.'

There was a silence. Ann waited, trying not to get into conflict with Meg, as she was a key witness and needed the woman to trust her.

'You're right—I'm sorry—I shouldn't have rushed in like that. I was just so desperate to warn Patty about what that mongrel is capable of. At least you have another key witness as well as Eddie now.'

'It's okay, Meg. Let's wait and see what this week brings if he returns. I just hope he hasn't already disappeared.'

Chapter Twenty-seven

Two months later

Ann threw her hands in the air. 'I can't believe it! What kind of justice system have we here?'

She and Tim were busy swapping notes as they left the court after Lyle's trial.

Ann continued, 'We should be celebrating and not commiserating.'

Tim took the glass of apple cider Ann handed to him. 'I feel the same way, Aunty. It just doesn't seem right. Men like him always have powerful lawyers, and money spells influence in this game—that's for sure.'

Ann poured herself a drink and joined him in the lounge. 'So, he is out on a suspended sentence for eighteen months and one hundred hours of community service. Humph! The snake has slipped through the net again. He probably thinks he'll be let off with good behaviour.'

'What a laugh he has to reside at his flat until he buys a house,' mocked Tim. 'It's so good he had to pay Meg compensation for the harm he caused and give her his share of the house.'

'Don't worry about that, Tim. The swine purchased the house with Meg's inheritance after they married, anyway. He'll trip up some more, before long—every dog has its day. And with Meg's restraining order in place, she'll be able to start a whole new life away from here, now their home has been sold.'

Ann looked at her watch. 'That reminds me— I told Meg I would talk to her today. She wants me to explain a few things about Lyle's conviction, so after we finish our drinks I'll call her. She's seething that he got off with such a light sentence.'

Tim rolled his eyes. 'I don't blame her. It doesn't seem fair that he appears to be walking away scot-free.'

'Believe me—give a loose cannon like Lyle enough rope and he'll hang himself. Eighteen months is a long time to keep his nose clean. He'll screw up, wait and see.'

***

Meg had invited Ann to join her for morning tea at their favourite café in Cockle Cove village. It was a lovely setting where Ann preferred to take clients for initial meetings.

When Ann spotted Meg, she noticed the once timid young woman was no longer the butterfly with crushed wings that she knew when they first met. The person before her wore a stunning blue off-the-shoulder summer dress with high-heeled shoes to match. Her thick, brown wavy hair had been coiffured and her face had come alive—a picture of health and self-confidence.

The two women hugged, and Meg insisted on buying morning tea to thank Ann for sticking by her.

'You've got to see my lovely new townhouse near here. I have a terrific view.'

'That's sounds wonderful—where is it exactly?'

'Not far from you in Cockle Cove village. I thought I might feel a little more secure knowing I have you living nearby and Detective Inspector Bryce Drummond pretty close too.'

Meg's announcement surprised Ann. She wouldn't normally want ex-clients living under her nose, but she'd become a friend for whom Ann had developed a real soft spot. Perhaps because she'd known her in the past.

'I needed to get away from Langhome, regardless that Lyle doesn't live there now. Do you know where he resides? Although I have a restraining order against him, I still want to make sure I keep right out of his way.'

'I'm sorry, Meg—I can't divulge that personal information. Perhaps there are mates of his who know where he lives—like that fishing friend who sheltered him after he left you.'

'I doubt that any of them would tell me— they'll be as shifty as he is.'

Ann wanted to know all about Meg's new life and tried to keep their conversations as positive as possible.

Meg's mood lifted. 'I've just started working for myself and have already set up a business teaching painting at a few colleges and art centres. It'll give me enough money to live on and I'm mortgage free.'

'Goodness, how did you manage that—the finances, I mean.'

'Lyle had to give me his half-share of our property as compensation for forcing me out of my home. He is still living off the royalties from his drone manufacture, but he probably won't get any more contracts from his usual customers. Seeing his name splattered across the internet and the papers naming him as a criminal will probably put them off having anything to do with him.'

'Well, Meg. He has well and truly cooked his own goose, that's for certain. Perhaps your lawyer can get the court to transfer the drone business over to you.'

'No, thanks. I don't want anything to do with it. That would give me nightmares.'

Meg sat wringing her fingers, eager to prise more information out of Ann.

'Please tell me, Ann, if you know. What is this Community Service that Lyle's doing to serve his sentence? What does it entail?'

'It can involve a number of things—but in Lyle's case, he has been placed in a work party to remove graffiti from buildings and fences. The men must also mow lawns and clear bush in designated areas.

Meg gave a wry smile. 'At last he'll have to pay the price for years of abuse and won't be in control. I just wish he were dead!'

Ann frowned at the remark, as she didn't expect Meg to come out with that. It was apparent that the poor woman still harboured a great deal of resentment towards her persecutor.

They finished their morning tea and Ann promised to visit Meg in her new home sometime soon.

Just as Ann said her goodbyes and headed for the door of the café, Meg stopped her.

'Wait!' Her hand dived into her handbag and produced a large envelope. 'This is the sum of money which the court had ordered Lyle to pay me for damages, which I promised you.'

Ann was taken aback as she took the envelope and peered inside. There was a business card with Meg's contact details and a huge wad of one hundred-dollar bills. Deciding to wait until she was alone before counting it, Meg turned to walk to her car.

Ann stopped her. 'Just a moment—there's something else I need to raise with you.'

Meg's smile disappeared.

'Don't worry, there's nothing wrong. It's just that the business of all Lyle's domestic abuse towards Eddie, Patty and you has been brushed aside for this bigamy case. I know you're relieved to be free of that marriage, but it still needs to be addressed. Although you're both separated, his Community Service for the Courts will fly by, and he'll then be able to roam anywhere without being punished for what he has done to you all.'

Meg tensed, her nose wrinkling.

'What are you saying?'

'I mean, with the help of you and the other girls, we can still convict him of severe family violence including grievous bodily harm with the evidence we have collected from you all.'

'How do we do that?'

'You leave it to me and my colleagues. We need to discuss this with Eddie and Patty and then arrest him.'

'Why didn't you do that before? I thought it would have been all dealt with at once during the hearing for the bigamy.'

'No, it doesn't work like that. Sorry, Meg. The cases are handled separately. I just wanted you to be free of the marriage so you could start again—and now you are.'

The women embraced, and Meg waved her off, beaming from ear to ear. 'Thanks for everything. Don't forget to drop by my new home soon.'

'I'll be in touch after I speak with the others,' said Ann, giving her a wave.

Sitting back in her vehicle, Ann felt overwhelmed by Meg's generosity, as she counted each hundred-dollar bill. This client, who, had now become a friend, had paid her far more than the price Ann had quoted. Meg had given her the first half at the beginning of the case and only had a thousand dollars left to pay, but the amount in the envelope was double that.

Just seeing the change in the woman's countenance and the smile on her face was enough for Ann. The police remunerated her services well, so she wouldn't have been out-of-pocket if Meg didn't have the money to complete the transaction. But perhaps by blessing Ann, Meg had also been rewarded.

Chapter Twenty-eight

Rex, the probation officer, sat with Bryce discussing complaints against Lyle during his Parole.

'We're getting a bit fed-up, to be honest,' Rex muttered. 'He has clever alibis for his absences when questioned, but without a monitored ankle bracelet we can't keep track of his every move.'

Bryce's eyes narrowed. 'What do you want me to do?'

'I don't know. But this fellow would have been better behind bars—if you want my opinion. He's an arrogant tyke.'

'I agree, he seems to come out of the crap smelling like roses.'

Bryce leaned on his desk in deep thought and opened the file that lay before him.

'So, what do you think about these charges Calamity Unlimited intends to bring against him?'

'You mean the two detectives, Ann and Tim?'

'Of course—they want me to arrest him for GBH and coercive control against his two wives. Unfortunately, although physical abuse leaves visible marks, psychological damage from intimidation doesn't and is much harder to prove, as you know.'

'What can you do then?'

Bryce pointed to a folder on his desk. 'We have sufficient medical evidence from Meg's doctor and her neurologist to interview him at the station for physical assault and go from there.'

'If I were you, I'd let him serve more of his current sentence in the community and before he finishes, lay that one on him. We've got him cleaning graffiti off walls and fences right now, and then he'll be cutting scrub up in the Ranges. I had hoped it would bring him down a peg or two and rid him of some of his arrogance.'

'The trouble is, with Community Service as a sentence—he's still free to come and go. Home Detention may have been better for him. Now, I need to speak to Ann and Tim, and then bring him in. I'll let you know, but it will be soon.'

***

Living on her own after years of married life, took Meg some getting used to. Although she was enormously relieved to no longer be the hostage of a sadistic tormenter, she was still nervy about living in her new brick townhouse by herself. She knew Lyle was now living far enough away in the bush somewhere in the Ranges, but her acute stress reaction still made her jumpy.

Shortly after moving in, Meg hired an electrician to install video surveillance cameras in and around the house, including a couple of panic buttons which were connected to a megaphone on the roof. She wasn't too good at managing them, as she found technology challenging, but it did make her feel a little more secure. The neighbours on either side were warm and friendly.

The week after she had shifted in, she was sure that Lyle's face had appeared for an instant when opening the blinds to investigate tapping on the glass pane. At first, she thought it was the branches of a nearby tree waving in the raging storm, but that was set too far back.

Another evening—footsteps had echoed on the deck, but no-one came to the door and knocked.

Then, as she closed the curtain, a face moved across the window and then vanished. Again, Meg was sure it was Lyle, but brushed it off, telling herself she was having flashbacks, just like those she'd suffered in the past.

She remembered Ann had suggested getting an ex-police dog as a companion—offering to help her find one. Years of harassment from Lyle had left her edgy. Perhaps it would settle down in time, but for now, she decided to phone Ann and let her know she'd decided to go ahead with acquiring a retired police dog.

After the phone call, Meg felt more settled knowing she'd soon have a house companion and could even meet up with Ann occasionally for a coffee and tell her about her insecurities.

She sat on her couch thinking about the other women Lyle had damaged. Eddie had given a remote witness interview from Australia during his trial and did not want to return to New Zealand while Lyle was still walking free, although he was serving a sentence in the community. Eddie's father and sister were still living in Australia, so it was unlikely she would return here, Meg thought.

Meg had been surprised to meet Eddie's father Jonathan in court, where he had also given a witness statement. She had talked at length with him after the trial and he offered to pay for her airfares to Brisbane if ever she wanted to visit Eddie at any time.

Perhaps when everything settles down, she could take that trip to Brisbane but first would have to apply for a passport as she hadn't used one in years—not since before marrying Lyle. That was another restraint he'd placed on her—further restricting her freedom. He just wouldn't allow it.

Meg and Eddie had plenty of stories to share with each other about their marriages to Lyle, and both completely understood the depth of pain they each had suffered at the hands of this merciless monster.

But poor Patty—the bully nearly ruined her life too, although she'd escaped by the skin of her teeth. It was time for Meg to pay her another visit, as she knew the girl was nervous that Lyle was still not behind bars.

Chapter Twenty-nine

Patty was thrilled to see Meg for the first time since Lyle's bigamy trial, and once again the girls sat in the garden in her landscaped backyard.

'I'm sure Lyle has been stalking me too,' said Patty. 'I'm not keen on being here alone at night anymore, although he hasn't got anything to gain from harming me.'

Meg repositioned her sunhat after the warm summer breeze lifted it slightly. 'Why would he stalk you?'

'He bumped into me in the village and asked if we could meet up. He said it was really important.'

'Don't you have a restraining order against him as I have?'

'No—I didn't see the need for it at the time.'

'Did you see him then?'

'I didn't bring him to the house. We met in a local café and he begged me to change my witness statement about the abuse, fabricating all kinds of excuses to make me have pity on him.'

Meg's eyes widened. 'You won't do that, will you? He must think we women are idiots.'

'No, I won't, but he's being really persistent—stating that our incompatibility and the short time we were together didn't warrant him getting a prison sentence. Of course, that was just a smokescreen—his denial of the abuse and trying to make me feel guilty.'

'Was he driving an old white Ute?'

'Yep—I even photographed the registration number. That shows how much I trust him.'

Meg leaned over to look at the image.

'Yes, that's the vehicle he's driving now. Perhaps you should call the police. How does he manage to stalk you when he's doing Community Service each day?'

'His probation officer told me he has to work seven hours daily, and on the days when not at work, he must attend an anger management program. We met on the weekend, not during the week.'

'I wasn't going to say anything so as not to unnerve you, but I'm sure he is watching me from a distance when my blinds are open.'

Patty shuddered. 'Oh—that gives me the creeps. What do you think he is up to?'

'Trying to frighten me off so that I'll clear out of the area, or just to make my life a misery for the trouble I caused by getting him arrested in the first place. He has more to lose from the long and detailed witness statement I've given the police than anyone else's.'

'I wondered why he was stalking you. Now it makes sense.'

'Ann Grieves said that the police are going to try to convict Lyle for grievous bodily harm towards me.'

Patty started kneading her neck muscles, as if uncomfortable with the conversation.

'You're probably right, especially with the physical abuse he used to harm you.'

'Yes, but his psychological cruelty is just as bad, except no one can see the scars. Anyway, I wanted to check out something, which is the main reason for my visit.'

Patty's eyes widened. 'Sure—fire ahead.'

'Are you certain Lyle didn't hit or use physical force on you in any way?'

Patty's face dropped as her eyes lowered.

'If he did, please tell me—it could get him a prison sentence, which means he'd be less likely to harass either of us again or damage another partner.'

'There was ... one occasion when he drove the car dangerously in a temper.'

Meg felt for Patty as her voice broke up. 'Please carry on.'

Patty pulled herself together. 'One day, while I was texting my sister in Australia that we were going to one of her favourite beach spots, Lyle insisted that I stop using my phone while in his company. He said it was rude, but he did that all the time.'

'Such a control freak! He behaved like that whenever I communicated with anyone on the phone and would pull it out of my hands. In the end, he cut me off from my friends.'

Patty continued telling her story. 'I replied that I was texting my sister, who was asking what I was doing that afternoon. He roared at me, demanding I put my phone away, but I refused.'

'Good for you!'

'He drove recklessly, focusing on me and not the traffic. Then he leaned over, snatched my phone, and smashed it against the dashboard. He really frightened me.'

Patty hesitated before she finished telling Meg all.

'As he continued driving on the narrow coastal road—still in a rage—he unexpectedly slammed on the brakes, forcing me to lurch forward in my seatbelt. My neck hurt badly. When I sought medical attention the next day, I was diagnosed with a serious whiplash injury.'

Meg sighed. 'More of what I experienced, too. Why didn't you order him out of your house and send him down the road?'

'For the same reason you didn't tell him to leave when he abused you.'

Meg looked at her disapprovingly. 'But we were married, and that was his home. He was hardly going to leave.'

'You could have gone to a woman's refuge centre for support.'

Meg took her hand. 'I'm sorry, Patty. We were both victims of coercive control, as that detective, Ann Grieves told me, and we were probably in denial of the severity of his behaviour—justifying it. For me, it was over and over, so I understand. I wasn't judging you.'

'That's okay. Let's stick together and I'll also give strong witness statements about the physical abuse for the charges the police want to bring against him for all of this.'

'His first wife, Eddie, spoke to me over the phone from Australia before Lyle's trial for bigamy. You'll be shocked at what he put her through.'

'Bad was it?'

'Yes, and none of it came out during the bigamy hearing, but it will if he goes to trial for Grievous Bodily Harm.'

'Can you tell me what she said?'

'I guess so—it'll all come out in court, anyway. When she announced she was pregnant with his child, he didn't believe it—accusing her of playing around—and kicked her in the belly. She rushed off to the hospital for a scan, scared of losing the baby, but it was safe.'

'What happened after that?'

'She gave birth to a healthy girl. Her sister and father helped her to recover and with raising the child.'

Patty let go of a loud sigh. 'I feel sick listening to that story—it's terrible. We can't let him get away with it and must pull together. Will she give evidence about that—do you think?'

'She has already written a statement about all the abuse and given it to Tim. They'll use it in court, but I don't think she'll appear. Her father, Jonathan, may come, as he attended my bigamy hearing.'

Meg picked up her bag, ready to leave. 'Eddie has spoken at length with me over the phone since the trial and keeps inviting me to stay. Her father is keen to pay for my airfares, but I'll have to wait until after Lyle's next court appearance.'

Patty scowled. 'It seems forever that we're waiting to start our new lives. He'd better go to prison this time, surely.'

Meg wrapped her arms around her before walking off. 'We reap what we sow in this life, and so will he—just wait and see.'

Chapter Thirty

When Patty's father, Michael Gregg, had initially received the news that his daughter's fiancée, Lyle Doyle, had two wives already, he exploded. It took Patty much convincing to keep him from unleashing his anger on Lyle, as she didn't want him going to prison for murder. Once Lyle had been arrested and charged with bigamy, Michael settled down, until he heard from Patty that the fiend had been stalking her his daughter.

'Where does he live—I'm going to pay him a wee visit?' he snarled when Patty dropped in on him.

'I don't know, Dad, and you can't just go rushing in like that—think of me, too. He's going back to court for charges brought against him for GBH towards me and the other two women. He'll probably do time for that, but I don't want you to get locked up, too.'

Michael started pacing the floor. 'Wait until I get my hands on him. I'm going to let him know I'm going to wreck his future, just as he has ruined others.'

'Sit down and relax, Dad. Let's just see the outcome of his next hearing first. By the way—I was wondering if you'd like to meet Meg—she's coming for dinner tomorrow night.'

Michael slumped back into his chair. 'Great idea—I've been waiting to meet her, but you kept putting it off.'

'I just didn't want you to discuss Lyle with her while still so raw, as she experienced far more trauma than I did.'

'Well, it would be nice to meet her.'

'Before dinner, Meg's going to help me plant some roses on the edge of the cliffs in the backyard, and I offered her one of my Agapanthus plants to dig up and take home.'

'I keep telling you to get a fence put up there on the edge of that steep drop, as you don't know when the bank will just give way. There is already a great deal of erosion on the edge.'

'Oh, Dad—you worry too much. I'll see you tomorrow around five unless you want to come earlier.'

'Great, see you then.'

✳✳✳

Eddie's father, Jonathan Thorpe, arrived—weary from his flight from Brisbane early that morning, having had sleepless nights worrying about the plight of his daughter as well as his granddaughter Sophie. Although he had another week to wait for Lyle's upcoming trial, he wanted to get settled in well before, and get sufficient evidence from others to add to his witness statement.

Meg's sister had offered to accommodate him, as did Meg, but he didn't think it appropriate to stay with her and had booked a room at the Green Oasis—a popular Bed and Breakfast not far from Meg's new home. He planned to call on her during his visit. The rental car he'd ordered online awaited him at the guest house.

Jonathan knew he should have warned the two investigators, Ann and Tim, or the police detective, Bryce Drummond, that he was coming, but there was something inside that stopped him from doing it.

Although he arrived after the buffet was finished, Maggie, the hostess, was gracious enough to serve him a full breakfast and coffee. After a good rest in a comfortable room with pleasant décor, he perused the notes he had brought with him concerning the trial.

He was desperate to talk to Lyle before the trial, and perhaps this was his only chance at tracking him down.

***

Tim arrived late at the early morning meeting instituted by Bryce. He'd received a phone call on the way out the door, and then there was a traffic jam in the village. Fortunately, the two detectives had waited for him before they began their review of the evidence they'd prepared for Lyle's trial.

'Tim—you're here, at last. We've already had coffee, and it's getting too late for any further holdups. Let's just get on with it.'

'Sorry, Bryce, but I was on the phone gathering more information from a key witness.'

'I see—you're leaving it a bit behind schedule, but better late than ever, I guess.'

Why would he give the gathering of evidence a schedule—weird! Tim detected a hint of annoyance in Bryce's voice and quickly opened his briefcase, pulling out the relevant documents, placing them on the desk. He kept quiet to allow the DI to have the floor, who expounded on the multiple types of evidence the police had to present in court. When he finished,

Bryce asked Ann what information she and Tim had gathered in addition to him. Thirty minutes later, he turned to Tim. 'Let's hear what you have to say ... you said you were busy with a key witness.'

Tim cleared his throat. 'Jonathan Thorpe is here. He didn't let us know, but his daughter, Eddie, phoned me to say her father left at the crack of dawn this morning on a flight to Auckland, and she's worried about what he might do.'

Bryce's thick eyebrows snapped together. 'What do you mean—might do?'

'She's concerned he has such a vendetta for Lyle that he could do something stupid.'

'Jonathan's not the only person bearing a grudge. Lyle has gained many enemies over the years,' muttered Ann.

'Mmm,' Bryce replied. 'Perhaps you could pay him a visit, Tim and give him a caution. Did she say where he was staying? We'll need to know that.'

'Yes—he's at the Green Oasis in the village.'

Bryce closed his dossier. 'Great! Report back if any problems arise.'

Ann hesitated while Bryce got to his feet. 'Perhaps we need to do the same with Patty's father, Michael. He's all riled up too, threatening all sorts if Lyle gets another light sentence.'

Bryce gathered up his files. 'I found him a rather placid man when I interviewed him. Hard to imagine him capable of hurting a fly.'

Ann shook her head. 'It's not what Meg told me. She said during their phone conversation that Patty told her he went ballistic when she announced that Lyle had two wives already. Michael threatened to kill him.'

Bryce's eyes squinted over the top of his metal-framed glasses as he glanced up from his notes. 'Oh, did he now? You're right, Ann—he has plenty of enemies. I can remember you told me Meg had muttered a few threats like that, too. The blighter has hurt a lot of people.'

Bryce looked at his watch. 'Sorry, team, I need to move on. I've another complex case I'm dealing with at the same time. Please keep in touch with your witnesses, and if there's any sign of trouble, call me.'

Ann tapped Tim's elbow as they headed towards her vehicle in the car park. 'You'd better see if you visit Jonathan this afternoon at the Green Oasis. Make sure he stays out of Lyle's way.'

Ann pulled out of the driveway of the police station. 'I'll visit the two girls, Meg and Patty, today, to make sure they haven't had any further trouble from Lyle. He's still on the roam until his trial, unfortunately.'

Tim scoffed. 'That says a fat lot of good about the justice system in New Zealand. How will the villains learn anything by these light sentences? And what about the impact on the victims?'

Ann chuckled to herself. 'I totally agree—and like I said, you should have stuck with a career in the police force. You could be in the CIB, like Bryce, making monumental overdue changes.'

'Ann—I'm taking off now.' Tim zipped up his leather jacket. 'I'll strike while the iron's hot and visit Eddie's father at the guest house, before he decides to play detective and get himself arrested. Eddie will be counting on me to keep an eye on him.'

'Why—what else did she say, other than him having a huge resentment towards Lyle.'

'Eddie told me her father is determined the rogue won't have anything to do with his granddaughter, Sophie. He's afraid that if he gets off on another non-custodial charge, that he may serve his sentence and then get powerful lawyers to help him get custody of his child. Eddie is terrified of that too—the swine has managed to contact her and threatened to do just that.'

Ann mulled over his words. 'That's not going to happen—with Lyle's history of domestic violence. But once he has served his time, he may still be granted access to Sophie. The courts don't like to see children denied contact with their parents.'

'That sounds horrific for Eddie, poor girl.'

Ann pulled into the station. 'Let's not get ahead of ourselves. One day at a time—but I do think we need to interview Jonathan now, too.'

'I know—I've been leaving messages on his phone to contact me, but he's not returning my calls.'

Chapter Thirty-one

Meg arrived at Patty's house soon after midday wearing a pair of denim shorts with a blue cotton top, spotty sunhat and leather sandals.

'Sorry, I'm a bit late. I had just seen Podge off for a day's outing with our neighbour, Peggy when Ann called unexpectedly—wanting to run over my victim impact statement to make sure I don't contradict myself in court.' She followed Patty through to the living room.

'Oh, really? Ann visited me too and left just before you arrived. It's strange, as she didn't phone to warn me, as she normally does.'

Meg frowned. 'Yes, that's unusual—what did she want with you?'

'Lyle's probation officer tipped her off that the rotter wanted me to change my witness statement. I'm sure she hoped to catch him here after learning that Lyle had planned to see me sometime today, and I think she may return again tomorrow. It's as if Ann suspects me of collaborating with him, but if only she knew how far from the truth that is.'

'What did you tell her?' Meg glanced at her in a scrutinising manner.

'I didn't mention that I'd met him at the local café but said he'd been sending texts to persuade me to change my witness statement. This made her furious. Lyle is in breach of his Suspended Sentence, so now Ann will contact his probation officer and the Court to have it nullified. It won't help his case for the trial, silly man.'

Meg rolled her eyes. 'He has a heightened sense of entitlement and thinks he's above the law.'

'Let's hope this breech will be added to his long string of other convictions.'

'I think I also put my foot in it with Ann.' Meg lowered her eyes sheepishly.

Patty rested her hands on her hips. 'What now? I hope it's not serious.'

'I'm not sure—it may undermine the reliability of my victim impact statement in court.'

Patty's eyebrows curved. 'What did you tell her?'

Meg stalled. 'I … said … I wished him dead. But it wasn't the only time I've said that to her when I was angry. It could be interpreted as me being jealous that he had another woman—in other words—vindictive. It may go against me during the trial.'

Patty nodded. 'Let me tell you—I wasn't exactly jumping for joy when you informed me that Lyle already had two wives. I could have killed him there and then. It's a natural reaction to an absolute betrayal of trust.'

'The detectives have a heap of dirt on him without our small slip-ups preventing justice being served.' Meg lifted her arm to squeeze a tense shoulder muscle. 'But let's be honest—we both want rid of the monster!'

She desperately longed for a break from this drama in her life. 'Let's drop the subject.'

Patty pushed the French doors wide open. 'Shall we go outside? It'll take your mind off it all before Dad comes and raises the ugly subject again. I hope Lyle doesn't arrive and completely ruin our evening meal.'

Meg put on gardening clogs she removed from the canvas bag hanging on her arm.

'I also have a skirt and top to change into before dinner later. What time did Lyle say he was coming?'

Patty glanced at the clock on the wall. 'He was overly casual about it and didn't give a time when he messaged me last—just said he would probably drop around sometime this evening.' She ducked back inside and returned with a shopping bag.

'A wee present from me to Lyle,' said Patty with a smirk on her face, holding open the bag so Meg could see the contents.

'Oh—I don't get it.' Meg's mouth turned downwards in disapproval.

Patty laughed. 'No, you don't understand. I'm just kidding, of course. It's not a gift—these are the things I'm going to return to him when he shows his face again—video cams he installed inside my home, his engagement ring and various pieces of jewellery and cards he used to keep me hooked in.'

'Good for you! Taking your power back again, I see. You'll feel so much better for doing it.'

'I have to see him first—that's if he still has the gall to turn up.'

They finished their drinks at the patio table and then wandered outside to the shed to collect up the gardening implements.

Patty picked up two pairs of gloves from a large orange bucket inside her shed while Meg wandered across the lawn to the garden. It was only a short distance from the eroding cliff edge with a two-hundred foot drop below. There was a waist-high box hedge as a border separating the lawn from the perilous cliff edge. The view of the sea was magnificent, and Meg could easily see why Patty lived there. Her house stood in a long row of other stately homes that lined the grass walkway on the edge of a public reserve bordering Clovelly cliffs. Some properties featured beautiful gardens—others extensive lawns, and several were secured by high fences and hedges. Between a few of these homes were grass alleyways that exited onto Clovelly Road. Patty lived at the far end of the walkway, which also ran parallel with the street.

'Here—put these gloves on.' Patty handed them to Meg after slipping on another pair.

Meg picked up the spade. 'I can dig the holes while you plant the roses and push the compost around them.'

'Sure, if you don't mind. Pity Dad isn't here yet. He could do the digging for us—except—I don't think he likes to get his hands dirty, being a seasoned office worker.'

Planting the roses took them the whole of the afternoon. Then Meg dug up a large Agapanthus and placed it into a bucket of water until she was ready to go home.

'There are more of these flowers growing wild by the clifftop path along the edge of the Reserve. If we go for a walk later, perhaps we can dig up a few other plants, discreetly.'

'Great, thanks.'

'Leave this one in the bucket, and when you go home, we can pack it with soil before you put it in the car along with any others we may find.'

At the end of the afternoon, after they finished their gardening activities, Patty showed Meg to a bathroom where she could clean up and change into fresh clothes.

When Meg had finished dressing, voices reverberated outside the door. Guessing Patty's father had arrived, she quickly pulled a comb through her hair and applied a spray-on deodorant under her arms, looking forward to meeting Michael, the illustrious Foreign Correspondent.

Chapter Thirty-two

By the time Meg had exited the bathroom, Patty was busy pouring her father a glass of wine in the lounge.

'Come and join us, Meg. A glass of white wine?' Patty held up the bottle.

'I'd rather have something without alcohol, thanks. It goes to my head too quickly and I'm driving.'

Patty's father stood up and put out his hand. 'Michael Gregg—pleased to meet you, Meg,' he said with a charming smile, before removing his black leather driving gloves.

'I'm pleased to meet you, too. Patty has told me so much about your remarkably interesting occupation.'

They all sat down in the lounge.

His charming smile revealed a set of sparkling white crowns. 'Interesting but hugely challenging at times.'

Patty poured a lime soda for Meg and handed around a plate of canapes.

Michael raised his eyebrows at Meg. 'I've heard that you have had some pretty shocking experiences that would leave some of my stories pale into insignificance.'

'Dad! I told you not to start,' Patty snapped.

Meg swung around to see the horrified expression on her friend's face.

'Don't worry, Patty. I'm used to the interrogation now, and it doesn't bother me to talk about it anymore. I've had Ann Grieves in my ear this morning discussing the trial and making sure I don't have any other evidence to add to my statement.'

Meg was amazed at the intensity of anger Michael vented regarding Lyle, even though Patty had escaped a nightmarish marriage—unlike her. He was obsessive and did not hold back from firing questions at Meg to compare her experience of abuse dished out by Lyle, with that of his daughter, Patty.

'Dad, please! Give the poor girl a break. She's been through enough already.'

Patty disappeared into the kitchen to rescue the roast chicken and vegetables, which had been baking slowly in the oven all afternoon. 'Dinner's ready—let's eat!'

Just as the girls began to dish up the food, Patty received a text. She stood in the corner of the kitchen and discreetly showed Meg, who pinched up her face. It was Lyle warning Patty he was running late but would still be coming before too long.

Meg craned her neck to see the text. 'Humph! I'll make sure I'm gone before he arrives—I don't want to see him!' she whispered.

'You girls need a hand out there?' Michael called from the lounge.

'No thanks, Dad. We're fine.'

Meg gave Patty a hand to serve the meal while Michael helped himself to more alcohol.

'Anyone else for a glass?'

Meg shook her head. 'I'll just stick to lime soda, thanks.' She flinched at the thought of him drinking and driving but said nothing.

Patty gave him a nod as he poured her another glass of wine. It was obvious Michael found it difficult to keep to any other topics of discussion other than Meg's marriage to Lyle. He became increasingly irate while he interrogated her about the abuse, while Patty continued to try to steer him away from that topic to no avail.

After the meal, the girls chatted in the kitchen clearing up, when Patty spoke softly to Meg.

'I'm so sorry about my father spoiling your evening. He's like a dog with a bone once he starts.' She switched on the elaborate coffee maker. 'I think he needs coffee.'

Meg shrugged. 'It's okay, don't be too hard on him—he has a good reason to be upset—but he undoubtedly has it in for Lyle. I'd hate to see them in the same room right now.'

'I agree. It would be interesting if we could all get together with Eddie and her father to swap notes. Imagine Lyle walking into a room with all of us.'

'I'd say his life wouldn't be worth living. Anyway—you might get a chance to find out soon. Eddie's father is expected to arrive this week.'

When the coffee machine had worked its magic, Patty leaned over to turn it off.

'Coffee's ready!' She carried the tray into the lounge and placed it on a side table.

Michael helped himself to a cup. 'It's such a lovely, warm summer evening. We could all go for a stroll along the pathway in front of your house, Patty.'

The path between the cliff edge and the houses was bordered by a makeshift fence instead of flora, in parts—separating the lawns from the steep drop to the shore below. But the rest of the path in the Reserve had no barrier except for weeds and overgrowth. It was a popular area, and walkers usually took time to admire particularly beautiful gardens featured in front of many of the grand homes.

Patty appeared unenthused. 'I'm a bit weary now, but perhaps Meg would like to go with you.'

Her other house guest only wanted to put her feet up and relax but realised the exercise would do her good. 'Perhaps a little later when my food has gone down, if that's okay. It doesn't get dark until nine.' She had taken that walk on previous visits with Patty.

Michael stood up to pour himself a second cup of coffee. 'That settles it, then. Let's play it by ear and see how the rest of the evening pans out.'

Chapter Thirty-three

Ann woke late the next morning with Scout standing next to her bed, holding his lead in his mouth. It was a new trick she'd taught him more recently.

'You'll have to wait, Scout. Let me take care of myself first, then it's your turn.'

Shuffling into the shower, rubbing her eyes and still feeling groggy, she heard her phone ring.

'Darn! I forgot to set my alarm. That'll be Tim waiting to hear from me,' she muttered.

Ann had said she would let him know her decision about bringing Lyle into the station for questioning. The culprit was in big trouble after breaching his probation order by collaborating with a key witness before his trial. If Ann was going to apprehend him, Tim wanted her to pick him up on the way.

She exited the bathroom and filled Scout's bowl with his special pellets, then changed the water in his bowl.

Before heading out the door to take the dog for his walk, she phoned Bryce for instructions.

'I'd like you to contact Lyle's probation officer and ask him to detain the rogue until you and Tim bring him in. If you have any trouble—call me.' Bryce finished the call.

Ann felt gut-wrenching guilt disappointing her faithful dog, but knew time was of the essence. She had an intuitive feeling all along that at some point during Lyle's eighteen-month suspended sentence—he was going to flee.

The look in her dear Beagle's eyes was enough to melt her heart, and she couldn't let him down.

'Tonight, boy—I promise you—I'll take you out. We have long evenings these days and there'll be plenty of time for a walk when I finish work.'

Ann phoned Lyle's probation officer and then Tim to say that she was on her way.

***

Tim hurried into the passenger seat when Ann picked him up at his gate. 'Where are we meeting Rex, his probation officer?'

'Down at Ashley Park. They're cleaning all the rubbish out of the creek today.'

'Oh, no, that means he'll stink your car out when we collect him.'

'I can always get one of Bryce's officers to accompany us and he can travel in that vehicle.'

When they arrived at the park, all they could see was Rex sitting on the grass with a group of men.

Ann pulled in alongside the creek and her eyes narrowed as she stepped out of the car and approached Rex. 'What's going on—where's Lyle?'

The officer stammered slightly. 'The men are taking a short break—I was just going to phone you. He hasn't turned up this morning. You'll have to go to his flat. Sorry, I should have checked before I arranged to meet you.'

'Humph!' Ann grunted. 'You're right about that. Why don't you go to his flat? It's your responsibility to monitor him.'

'I can't leave these men here unsupervised. Would you mind going? I can ring the station and arrange for a few officers to do it if you'd prefer.'

'No, we'll go. But I'll report directly back to you if he's not there.'

'Please tell me either way. I need to know his whereabouts, thanks.'

The detectives wasted no time tearing off to Lyle's flat. When they arrived, there was no sign of life. His blinds were drawn, but his Ute was gone.

'You've got Lyle's phone number, haven't you?' asked Tim.

'Yes, you're right. I'll try calling him.'

Ann rang his number. 'That's unusual—it just cuts off immediately. Perhaps he's charging it.'

'That shouldn't make any difference.'

'I'm going to call Bryce and let him know. He'll have to get police officers out tracking him and then I'll alert the airport.' Ann was aware of her cheeks turning red, with her senses heightening at the thought of hunting down a criminal—something she enjoyed as it made her feel alive.

'That's wise—he'll be off to the airport and on the next plane to who knows where, before you can say Jack Rabbit.'

Ann took her phone out of her jacket pocket. 'That's what concerns me. I'm going back home to collect Scout before we start looking for him.'

Tim gave her a bewildered look. 'Why is that?'

'Because he's the best tracking dog I've ever seen and has never let me down.'

Tim bit his lip and kept quiet.

'I'm thinking that because Lyle made many enemies, we could have a number of Persons of Interest. We need all the help we can get, and so does Bryce.'

'Where do we start, Aunty?'

'At the beginning. We need something of Lyle's, and a warrant to enter his flat could take too long. Perhaps Meg could help us.'

Chapter Thirty-four

Ann turned on her phone's speaker so that Tim could hear Bryce's news.

'You would not believe what's happened. We've just received a call from one of the local residents near Patty's home at Clovelly Heights. He was walking under the overhanging cliffs when his dog picked up the scent of a man lying on the sand whom he reported dead. I've already sent officers to take a look at the body, and they've identified him from his Driver's Licence as Lyle Doyle. An ambulance is on its way.'

Ann almost dropped her phone. 'This is incredible. I felt something was going to happen—more like Lyle doing a complete runner, but not this. Do you think it's suicide in view of the high chances of him going to prison this time?'

'I've no idea, but I'd like you and Tim to get down there as soon as possible please, as Forensics are heading to the beach now.'

Ann was delighted that Bryce sent her instead of taking control of the situation himself, although he was the Detective Inspector for Cockle Cove Police Station and the surrounding district that included Clovelly. He still treated her as though she was a DI currently working for the police, although she was not. Being self-employed as a private investigator had made no difference to Bryce in the way he perceived her, as she was still a highly respected, award-winning detective to him, as she was in the past.

***

Fortunately for those involved, the tide was still a distance back from the shore. It was a long hike for the forensic team to walk from the Clovelly Beach car park. Police officers had already cordoned off the area, and a few of them were asking inquisitive beach goers to move away out of the area.

When Ann and Tim arrived, investigative Police officers were scurrying around gathering evidence.

'Ah, here is the forensic team,' said Tim, standing back to let them through.

Lyle's broken body lay on his back on the beach under the overhang of the cliff face. Ann glanced upward to see how far he'd fallen.

She shuddered. 'I'd say with a drop that high he probably smashed every bone in his body.

While Tim stood with eyes wide, gaping at the cliff face, Ann approached the pathologist, who was busy swiping investigative crabs and lice off the corpse. She saw that Lyle's shirt was torn, probably from hitting rock and brush on the way down.

Ann pulled on a mask. 'James! I wondered if you were handling this. Nice to see you, except for the circumstances.'

He gave Ann a half-smile and placed his leather medical bag next to the victim—methodically examining the body from head to toe and then turned him over.

Tim joined them, donning his mask and squirmed at the sight of the victim's smashed skull, and the mangled leg which became visible when the coroner pulled back his jeans. The young detective yanked off his mask and retched as he ran to the bushes near the rocks and heaved, while Ann looked up in sympathy but stayed back, not wanting to render further embarrassment on him. He wiped his mouth with his sleeve as he tentatively walked back to the gruesome scene.

'It has been a while—sorry about that.'

Ann drew alongside and patted his shoulder. She handed him a fresh mask. 'We've all done it, and it never gets easy. I have to call Bryce back and give him a report when the pathologist has finished his initial examination.'

'James—are there any signs of foul play? I mean—the head injury? Some officers suspected suicide.'

The man in the white forensic bunny suit looked up. 'I can't be sure. The black bulge on his abdominal wall is a haematoma as a result of bleeding into the superficial tissues. It was likely caused by either a blunt instrument or a fist to his belly.'

'So, it's not likely to be suicide then?'

'No, I doubt it. Suiciders rarely dive off a height—they usually jump feet first. His leg injury would be from hitting a rock on the way down, by the look of the torn flesh. I think he could have been pushed backwards. I suspect he sustained spinal fractures, but that is difficult to know until I carry out an autopsy. I'm going to request to do it at the mortuary in the city Forensic Lab. I'll arrange it now.'

Before he was able to remove his gloves and pick up his phone, Ann questioned him again.

'Do you have an estimated time of death?'

'I would say last night—sometime close to midnight—between nine and twelve. I won't be able to confirm this until I have the lab results.'

While James made a number of phone calls, Ann rang Bryce to update him.

'Come on, Tim—let's go. Bryce wants to see us at the station,' she said, dropping her phone into her pocket.

They trudged through the sand back to the car park—a difficult trek, as the tide was on its way in. That part of the beach had already been cordoned off by the police officers who were interviewing people in the car park.

While Ann knew it would be a huge relief for the women who had been plagued by Lyle for years, she would hate to think that any of them had done something foolish and risked possible imprisonment. Although it was difficult for her to imagine anyone taking Lyle on after Meg told her that he had been a Judo expert in his younger days.

She and Tim had to get to the truth as fast as possible.

Chapter Thirty-five

The results from the pathology lab showed only Lyle's own DNA on his body and his clothing, except for the denim jacket he was wearing, which contained strands of hair which needed identification.

'If the hair was Meg's, it could have been acquired from the house she and Lyle had shared,' the pathologist explained. 'But I also found some strands tucked in the armpit area of the right sleeve of the jacket, and have no idea whose it could be, as it doesn't match the rest we found.'

Ann was relieved that the pathologist discovered nothing on Lyle matching Patty, as she believed the girl wouldn't hurt a fly. She had felt almost guilty about landing on her unexpectedly the day before, carrying out a humiliating interrogation. As if the poor girl hadn't gone through enough. Ann couldn't visualise her using a fist or object to inflict a sizeable wound to a man's belly. Nor could she see Meg doing it, either. Both girls appeared to be in the clear, so far. But this was a murder investigation, and it was Ann's responsibility not to take her foot off the pedal—something she learnt as a young detective.

'I'm relieved with the results, although it appears we have a long road to hoe with having to investigate all Lyle's enemies. Let's talk to our forensic pathologist. He has the reports ready for us.'

James and Ann had become good friends over the years, and he knew what to expect from her. She usually asked the same questions and was mostly predictable.

'So, what's the verdict?' Ann leaned over the pathologist's table.

James smiled. 'Just as I suggested—see here.' He pointed to a massive bruise on the victim's belly. 'A hard blow to the abdomen with a blunt instrument. He must have had his back to the edge of the bluff and plummeted backwards.'

'Wow, I'm trying to think who would have had the strength to push him over the edge. Six foot two he stood and a giant of a man at that—or at least compared to my shorter stature.'

'Or whack him so hard with an implement that he couldn't stay upright with the pain and stumbled back.' James always tried to get the upper hand with Ann and show how smart he was, which sometimes irritated her.

'True—that's food for thought. The blow may not have been intended to push him off the edge, but to teach him a lesson.'

James stood back and removed his gloves. 'That's the only evidence I can say gives me reason to suspect he was attacked. It's definitely not suicide.' He flipped through the first few pages of his report. 'Ah—here. There was no other DNA found on the victim's body or clothing, except strands of hair. It could be possible, seeing as he was married, they belong to his wife. You could bring some of her hair in to be matched. Nix else, I'm afraid. The needle in the haystack may be a lot deeper than you think.'

Ann was relieved but needed to get to work on finding conclusive evidence.

'Thanks, James. I'll be back again soon with more for you to test. I'd best get a move on and report back to Bryce.'

'Oh, so you're not entirely in command any longer—is the big DI watching over you now?'

'You've got it. That's the price I paid for becoming a free-lance private detective.'

'I hope it's worth your while.'

'It is—the Police pay me handsomely.'

'Wait—how about the dinner date you promised me last Christmas that never happened? What about tonight?'

Poor beggar. He never stops trying.

James and Ann used to be close colleagues and supported each other a great deal when her late husband Terry was still alive, and he had always treated her with great respect and admiration. She became isolated from many of her close friends after moving to Southland. James was another one with whom she'd lost contact.

'Sorry James, please don't take it personally—but my workload dictates my social life, as you know, and it's just too heavy right now. Perhaps once this case is over, we could meet for a drink—no promises, mind.'

Tim was at the police station talking to Lyle's probation officer when Ann texted him to meet her in the carpark.

'Thanks for coming, Tim. We must visit Meg and Patty to notify them of Lyle's death. But I'm sure it'll be relief—not grief—that Lyle has gone forever.'

'I don't blame them—poor women. They've both been through hell.'

Ann wondered if perhaps this gentler side to Tim was the real reason he left the police force to take up cybercrime—although he could fight like a dog when necessary.

'What did Rex have to say about Lyle's movements?'

Tim licked an index finger and flicked through the pages of his notebook.

'Rex had been concerned about Lyle's long absences for meal breaks—often returning late to join his work party in the afternoon, making lame excuses.'

Ann shook her head. 'Why didn't Rex bring him into the station for breaching his parole?'

'He was going to—but thought it didn't seem serious enough. He said Lyle would have been facing multiple allegations during his upcoming trial anyway.

'We know he was sneaking off to stalk the women who are witnesses for the trial. But there won't be a court case now, of course,' Ann murmured. 'We'll need the times he was absent though so we can tie it in with witness statements, as they could become suspects now.'

'He gave them to me—here.' Tim waved the probation report at Ann.

'Keep hold of it,' Tim. 'I hope it's just a copy, as Bryce will be looking for it.'

'Yes, Rex assured me.'

Chapter Thirty-six

Ann could see Patty's car in the driveway. It was her lucky day, as she pulled up outside her gate.

The young woman was delighted to see her and Tim, and there appeared to be no change in her usual congenial temperament, Ann thought. *Hard to imagine her as a killer but wonders never cease in this game.*

When Ann broke the news to her, Patty's eyes welled up, but it was obvious they weren't tears of grief. She took a deep breath and exhaled loudly.

'Well, I suppose I'm not the only person who is glad to see him gone—and I didn't have anything to do with this.'

Ann gazed with astonishment at her sudden defensiveness.

'We're not here to accuse you, Patty—just to inform you of his death and ask if you have any information that may assist our enquiries. We need to interview anyone who had contact with him the day he died. We may as well start with you, now we're here.'

It took a good hour to get Patty to give them a full explanation about the evening in question, when Meg and Michael were dinner guests—the conversations and their exact activities.

'So, you started out gardening together—you and Meg, around mid-afternoon. What time did your father arrive?'

Patty sat crumpling her dress. Her usual calm disposition disappeared suddenly. She didn't even offer them a drink, and Ann was parched.

'I can't remember exactly. I guess it would have been close to dinner time—around six. I remember thinking he knew we had the planting to do, but conveniently arrived right on meal time, as usual.' She gave Ann a half-smile.

Ann winked at Tim. 'I get what you mean— typical man, eh?'

Tim ignored the jibe. 'Patty, where did you do your planting with Meg?'

'Out on the back lawn by my box hedge.' She pointed towards the newly planted roses.

Ann held her black notebook, taking everything down. 'And you were only planting roses—is that all you were both doing in the garden that afternoon?'

'Yes, except for a large Agapanthus I told Meg she could dig up from my garden over there near the roses.'

As the detectives walked towards the gate, Ann paused. 'Your father—did he do any gardening with you yesterday?'

'No, he didn't. I told you he arrived later before dinner.'

'We'll be in touch when we've more information following our enquiries. Please stay in the area, Patty, until we have finished our investigation.'

'Am I a suspect?'

'Not at this stage, but we may need to question you again. I'll keep in touch.'

***

The curtains were drawn, and the townhouse appeared as though Meg had deserted it. The sun had disappeared behind the hills at the rear of her home, casting a shadow on the house. It usually happened around three each day and was one drawback Meg had mentioned to Ann about living in the native bush that surrounded Cockle Cove Village. Whereas Ann lived next to the beach and her home was a sun bath.

Meg's new Beagle dog barked, and then there was a face at the window as she drew the curtain aside. She smiled and waved, then rushed outside to greet Ann and Tim as they stepped out of the Land Rover.

'Come on in—you took me by surprise. I wasn't expecting anyone today.'

'We have some news about Lyle and need to ask you a few questions. Mind if we come in?'

Ann focused her gaze on Meg's body language. She knew her well by now and was accustomed to her being noticeably flustered due to her high anxiety, but today she was particularly calm, which Ann thought odd, and then she realised—Meg felt secure and relaxed with her new canine protector.

The afternoon tea offered by Meg, Ann surprisingly turned down and was eager to get on and track down all the other Persons of Interest on their list.

'I hope you don't mind, but we have other people to interview. Perhaps soon I can visit you on my own for some girls' time, but before that, I have upsetting news.'

Meg's face dropped as she froze.

'I don't know how to put this, Meg. We've not come on a light-hearted note, as we're here to tell you that Lyle is dead. I'm sorry to say we have evidence to suggest he may have been murdered.'

Meg lurched forward, placing her mug of tea onto the coffee table. It spilled out everywhere.

'Doesn't matter—it has gone cold, anyway. I made it before you arrived.' She shook her head. 'I just can't believe Lyle's dead!'

Tim reached for the cup. 'Can I make you another cup.'

'No, that's kind of you, but I don't think I could drink it now—I've just lost my appetite.' She grabbed a handful of paper tissues from a box on the sideboard and mopped up the spill.

'Where did they find his body?'

'Under the cliffs overhanging the walkway in the Reserve. It was directly under the bluff that juts out in front of the high hedge by the grand Mediterranean-style home.'

'What exactly happened to him?'

Ann elaborated, detailing Lyle's injuries and the findings of the forensic pathologist.

'A blunt object, you say. Wow—that's pretty gruesome. I know I hated him, but that sounds awful.'

'I'm sorry to do this, Meg, but I need to ask you questions relating to yesterday afternoon when you visited Patty. She already told us you had been gardening—planting roses.'

'Yes, that's right. We were out the back in the garden and finished about five thirty. Michael arrived while I was getting into fresh clothes in the bathroom—just before Patty served up dinner.'

'She also said you had borrowed gloves and a short-handled spade from her. We need to take them in for testing please.'

Meg sat up stiff as a ramrod. 'Why is that?'

'We're using a process of elimination and gathering evidence.'

'But why me?'

'Because you had an axe to grind with Lyle, if you excuse the pun, and have a strong motive for wanting to get rid of him.'

Meg drooped, resting her head in her hands.

'Oh, no, not again. I was under suspicion when Lyle went missing while fishing—and now this.'

'I'll get the things you asked for—wait here,' she ordered. But the detectives ignored her request and followed her out to the garden, while she kept glancing sheepishly over her shoulder. Arriving at her corrugated iron shed, Meg pulled open the door and produced an ice cream container, pulling off the lid. It revealed a pair of newish, dusty leather gloves.

'That's an unusual place to keep them,' said Tim. 'Mind if I ask why you store them there?'

'To keep the bugs out. Things like wetas and cockroaches like to make comfortable homes in them. I clean forgot to return them to Patty.'

Ann chuckled. 'That makes sense. I've encountered that myself a few times. Would you mind letting me take them for examination? We'll need the short-handled spade you borrowed too.'

'I'm so sorry—with the looming court case and sleepless nights—I honestly forgot that I still had Patty's gardening stuff. I did intend to return them.'

Ann was amused that Meg was more concerned that she hadn't given her friend's things back than not disclosing to the police she had them. Perhaps she really was naïve.

'They'll be returned after Forensics has finished examining them.'

The detectives were careful when securing evidence and always wore gloves when handling anything that could be connected to a crime. Ann dropped the items into a plastic bag, ready for Tim to carry out to her car.

Meg's eyes were out on stalks. 'What now—are you going to arrest me?'

Ann heard the tremor in her voice. 'No, of course not. If you aren't guilty of any malicious act towards Lyle by pushing him over the edge of the cliff, you've nothing to worry about. We won't find his DNA on the gloves or spade.'

Meg breathed out heavily. 'That's a relief.'

She lowered her gaze and went quiet after suddenly having a flashback of Lyle floundering in the sea. Scenes like that still haunted her at times, particularly when she was stressed. *Was this yet another game of his?*

'There is something, though. Did you meet up with Lyle at all that evening on the walkway or elsewhere?'

'Goodness—you really do think I'm capable of dealing such a hard blow to his belly that he went flying off the bluff—unbelievable!'

Ann eye-balled her. 'You haven't answered my question.'

Meg swung around and glared at Ann. 'No, absolutely not! None of us went for a walk that evening—we were too tired. But on my way home, I stopped a little way down Patty's street to enter the Reserve. I took her spade and gloves to dig up one of the smaller Agapanthus on the cliff top walkway, just like she suggested. I'd parked the car by the fourth entrance to the Reserve near Patty's house, and I walked the whole length of the track and back again after digging up an Agapanthus. When I couldn't find any other plants that were suitable, I returned to my car and drove home.'

Ann scratched the side of her nose with her pen. 'What time was this?'

'Around eight … I think. The sun hadn't completely gone down, and it was light enough to walk there.'

'So, you were the only one who walked along the cliff tops that evening after dinner?'

Meg hesitated. 'I don't know about … um … never mind.'

'You mean Michael? Could he have gone off for a walk alone?'

Meg hesitated. 'I … um … I'm not sure.'

Ann spelled out to Meg that to withhold evidence, was perverting the course of justice for which she would be charged.

'I'm not sure what Michael did, as I left first. He said he would stay with Patty for a bit longer to talk.'

'I'll be questioning Michael, anyway. Did he say anything about Lyle during the meal?'

'He wouldn't stop ranting about him until Patty said to put a cork in it.'

'Did he make any threatening comments, such as what he might do if he got hold of Lyle?'

'I can't quite remember. But while Patty was dishing up the meal, she received a text message from Lyle, which she showed me and didn't want Michael to know.'

'What did it say?'

'He told her he had been delayed and would be there a little later than expected.'

'What time was that?'

'Just after six.'

'We'll be asking for Patty to hand in her cell phone—and sorry, we'll need yours, too. I'll give it back as soon as Tim has examined it.'

Meg grimaced. 'That is so humiliating! Not that I've got anything to hide, but all my private messages are there.'

Ann placed a hand on Meg's arm. 'Look, dear—unless you aren't telling us the truth, you have nothing to be afraid of. We'll get it back to you in the next day or two.'

'You reckon? The police are going to try to pin it on me. I know how they work.'

Ann gave her a half-smile. 'So do I, remember? I won't let them accuse you unless we have evidence to prove otherwise.'

Meg trudged into the kitchen to get her phone and begrudgingly handed it to Tim, who placed it in a bag.

'That's my new iPhone which Angela and Pete kindly gave me.'

'Thanks, Meg. Now—if you could lastly give Tim your phone's security code, and then two or three strands of your hair for forensic testing—we'll be out of here.'

'I don't use a code key,' Meg grumbled, pulling a small handful of hair from her head and thrusting it at Tim. He placed it in another evidence bag.

Ann placed a hander on her shoulder. 'One more thing, I'm sorry. We'll need the clothing you wore in the Reserve the night you had dinner with Patty and Jonathan.'

Frustration crinkled Meg's eyes. 'I hope that's all!' She scurried off into her bedroom.

The dog began to make a din, whining in the laundry. Having given the detectives the hair samples and clothing, Meg let him into the lounge. He licked Ann half to death before he obeyed his owner's order to lie down.

'He probably smells Scout on me. It will be interesting to get both dogs together sometime. I'll bring him over one day soon.' Ann made a fuss of Meg's new companion. The dog then sniffed at Tim and welcomed him as a friend.

Ann leaned over and rubbed the dog's belly as he lay on his back. 'I see that this wee fellah is settling in well. I'm so glad you agreed to take Scout's brother.'

'Oh, he is marvellous—such a wonderful companion. He won't let anyone near me unless I tell him it's okay. That's why I shut him in the laundry, but he could hear you.'

'What did you end up calling him in the end?'

'I didn't like his kennel name, so he is now my Podge—see the size of his tummy.'

Ann grinned. 'Plenty of good walks will get rid of that. Now—I'm going to send these items to the lab by urgent courier for testing. The faster we do that, the sooner you can relax. I'll be in touch with you soon.'

Chapter Thirty-seven

Driving to the police station, Ann was unsettled about Meg's mental state.

'I've never seen her that jittery—not since I first broke the news to her about Lyle's bigamy.' Ann adjusted her sun visor. 'She was really on edge when we told her he'd been murdered.'

Tim nodded. 'I know exactly what you mean. I noticed the extreme change in her body language too.'

'Do you think Meg's hiding something? I wouldn't have thought her capable of attacking Lyle—she was terrified of him.'

Tim pulled out a chewing gum packet from his trouser pocket and offered it to Ann before he slid one into his mouth.

'No, thanks, I don't touch the stuff. It gets caught on my partial plate.'

Tim chuckled. 'It'll be interesting to see how the forensic test on Lyle's denim jacket pans out.'

'That's why we need to get to the station and send these things off to the lab.'

Ann pulled into the station's carpark where they headed straight to the forensic lockup to deposit Meg's hair samples. They included Patty's spade and gloves, which would all be sent to the lab by urgent courier.

***

Two days later

Ann hurried along the corridor of Cockle Cove Police Station with Tim in tow. She tugged on his sleeve. 'Come on—let's see if we can find Bryce. He'll have the report from the search team who initially scoured the cliff top. I hope they haven't found anything that could connect either Meg or Patty with Lyle's death. It would be ghastly to discover that either of them is implicated in his murder in any way.'

Bryce met them as he was leaving his office. 'Ah—my two musketeers. I was about to phone to see how you'd got on with interviewing the two women.'

'That's why we're here. Are you heading off?' asked Ann.

'Not really—it's just that I haven't had a proper meal break today and was on my way to our café. Would you like to join me?'

Ann threw Tim a glance. 'How about it—do you need to be anywhere else today?'

'No, I'm fine. I've got some stuff to do tonight for the bank—other than that, I'm free for the rest of the afternoon,'

Bryce was his usual generous self. Whenever Ann was around, he insisted on shouting her lunch. She wasn't sure if it was just a chivalrous gesture, or whether he was still trying to win her over—just as her local church vicar, Thomas, still persisted in doing.

'Lunch is on me, unless you have eaten already.' He directed them to take a place in the queue at the station's canteen.

'Oh, alright. I still haven't perfected the skill of saying *No* to you.'

Bryce winked at Tim, as they both amused themselves with jovial banter.

At the table, Bryce filled their glasses with water from a carafe. 'We still have no leads on who could have killed Doyle,' said Bryce.

Ann finished buttering her muffin and licked her fingers. 'No, but there are a number of

Persons of Interest with plenty of motive for murder.'

'Some concerns have come to light following the forensic testing of the items you gathered from Patty Gregg's property. We'd better go back to my office to discuss these after we've finished eating.'

While Ann topped up her Earl Grey tea from the stainless steel teapot, her brain did cartwheels as she mulled over what could be amiss with the items she and Tim had collected from Patty and Meg. They'd initially cleared them of any DNA from Lyle. She shuddered at the thought of either women being involved in his death.

Bryce wiped his hands on a paper napkin and stood up. 'Well, team—shall we move on to my cave? I need to process this new information I've received.'

Tim bolted the remnants of his meat pie, wiped the residue of tomato sauce from his mouth and followed after Bryce and Ann. He moved up alongside the DI. 'I'm keen to see what you have for us—thanks for lunch—by the way.'

'Yes, thanks, my friend—it's our turn to do the honours next time.' Ann followed the men as they walked into Bryce's office, where he pulled the reports from a drawer in his desk and opened the file.

'Soil from Patty Gregg's gloves was found on the walkway by our search team near the spot where Lyle fell. Forensics has confirmed this. I sent officers—upon receiving these results—to obtain a soil sample from Patty Gregg's garden where Meg had used the gloves. It matched soil debris that was found at the crime scene. Did she give you an explanation for this?'

Ann cleared her throat. 'Patty has provided us with an alibi for the soil from her garden being found on the cliff top walkway near the crime scene. She said Meg had been there, digging up a shrub from the cliff edge. I was about to submit my report.'

Bryce nodded. 'I see—and now I would like you to pay Michael Gregg a visit. It seems he was livid with Lyle about betraying his daughter, you told me. I want you to document his exact movements that evening—particularly what time he arrived and left her home.'

Ann relished having red herrings thrown into a crime investigation, and they often occurred when they encountered a stalemate in progressing the case.

'We'll get onto it right away.'

Bryce's expression hardened. 'You'd better come up with more concrete evidence. We've plenty of motives and Persons of Interest, but without real proof, we've lost the battle before we've started.'

Ann tapped him on the shoulder as they left his office.

'I won't let you down—promise.'

Chapter Thirty-eight

This time, Patty was much more tense than on their previous visit. Ann hadn't divulged over the phone the real reason for their meeting—only they'd like to ask her a few more questions.

The detectives waived the offer of coffee from Patty when they entered her home, as they needed to cut to the chase.

Tim sat with pen in hand, ready to take notes, while Ann did the questioning.

'Can you remember what everyone was wearing that evening?'

Patty began to pick at her fingernails. 'Meg arrived in denim shorts with a blue cotton top and wearing sandals. She had also brought clothing to change into before dinner and rubber gardening clogs.'

Ann glimpsed at Tim, making sure he was getting it all down in his notebook.

'Can you describe that?'

'Meg changed into a kind of beige linen skirt with a white tee shirt and walked around the house in bare feet.'

'What about your father?'

'He wore jeans and a red check shirt. On his feet he had brown leather shoes.'

'Wait a moment—if you don't mind. I just need to catch up.' Tim wrote frantically and flicked over to the next page. 'Continue please.'

Ann fired another question at her. 'Did he bring a bag with him?'

'No, but I gave him a shopping bag with vegetables from my garden, which he took when he left to go home.'

'What time was this?'

'Around eleven. Meg had already left by then.'

Ann gave Tim a nudge and gathered up her things. 'Patty, we need to get off now, as my dog is sitting in the car. I brought him along to do some tracking along the cliff top around the crime scene. But before we go, I'd like to take your cell phone to examine those texts of Lyles. I promise that one of us will drop it back to you first thing in the morning.'

Patty appeared hesitant. *Is she hiding something?* Ann wondered.

Patty's nose twitched like a frightened rabbit. 'I'm not sure. I don't feel so secure without my phone—I haven't got a landline.'

Ann's eyes darted to Tim. 'Would you be able to inspect her phone back at the station and return it to Patty before the evening?'

Tim gave her a half-smile and didn't exactly jump at the idea. But he realised, that the girl was particularly vulnerable now.

'I don't use a code key or PIN number—you can get straight in without one,' Patty said abruptly. She handed Tim her phone.

The detectives excused themselves and started out on their next plan of action—examining the cliff-edge near the crime scene.

***

Ann parked on the road next to the fourth entrance where Meg said she'd dug up a plant. Scout dived off the back seat of the car, heading straight for the nearest bush after Ann opened the car door, pulling on his leash. She felt guilty that he'd been in the vehicle far too long. But now she had work for him—just what he'd been born to do.

'Here Scout!' He raced over to her and promptly emptied the bowl filled with water from her pump bottle, which she always kept in her car.

She leaned back into her boot again and took out a bag. 'Tim, put these on.' Ann slipped on rubber gloves before handing a pair to him.

'Thanks—where shall we start?'

'Wait, a moment. I need to give him the scent.'

Ann bent over and rubbed Meg's clothing under Scout's nose, commanding him to track.

'Where exactly did Meg dig up the plant? Perhaps we need to see how close it is to the crime scene.'

Tim licked his thumb and flicked through a few pages of his notebook. 'Meg drew me a small diagram of the area. She entered the walkway at the fourth entrance to the Reserve near Patty's home between the houses with the tall hedges— about here—after parking her car on the road and began walking down slowly looking for plants.'

'Let me see the map. Ah—there it is.' Ann pointed to an area on the cliff several metres from where they stood. It was the spot Meg had described where she'd removed the Agapanthus plant. 'Let's check it out.'

Within minutes, they discovered the location. The cavity had been filled in with fresh soil and a small amount surrounded the hole.

'Meg was a long distance from the crime scene here. Let's walk further along the rest of the path.'

When they arrived at the cordoned area where Lyle had fallen, Ann scanned the homes and could see that no one could have clearly witnessed the attack on him, as the nearby houses stood behind tall hedges.

'This is a fair distance from where Meg dug up the Agapanthus back there.' Tim paused to make notes.

Scout began tugging on his lead, as Ann released the line to give him full rein. He rushed directly to the edge of the walkway and halted then sat down—wagging his tail less than five metres from where Lyle fell.

Tim was amused. 'Looks like we didn't need Meg's diagram.'

'You're right. It appears she started digging around this plant here and then must have stopped. She pushed the fresh soil back around the plant before leaving the Reserve.'

Tim wandered over to check it out and photographed it.

Ann stood on the spot circled within the cordoned area and froze—pointing. 'It's a long way down there.'

Tim joined her and stood with hands on hips, surveying the area. 'That's why Lyle's body hurtled over the side. Further back, where Meg had begun digging, there's an outcrop of vegetation that could have broken his fall, but here there is nothing—only a sheer cliff.'

Ann inspected a nearby shrub.

'Tim, have you got your magnifying glass—the new one you bought last week?'

'Yep, I'm onto it. You want me to inspect the bush for fibres?'

'Yes, please. 'Scout is telling us he picked up Meg's scent, so she must have been at this spot too.'

Ann was about to think her Beagle had brought them on a wild goose chase, but she hated to doubt him, as he'd never let her down in the past.'

'Eureka! This is what he's showing us.'

Tim pointed to a tiny remnant of beige linen that appeared to match Meg's skirt.

'Let me see the garment,' Tim asked Ann, who was still holding Meg's clothes. 'See, this hem here has been torn slightly, and the stitching pulled out, but along with it a tiny cluster of linen fibres too.'

'Remarkable! Well, Scout, my boy. You have still got it, and you definitely aren't ready to go out to pasture.' She patted the dog and gave him a treat from her pocket. *I wonder why Meg had been down this end of the Reserve*, she pondered.

While Tim carefully documented the forensic evidence in his notebook, something else caught Ann's eye that sparkled in the sun. She bent over to take a closer look at another Agapanthus plant near the bush Tim was examining and saw a tiny object lying in the grass.

She picked up what appeared to be a silver earring with a greenstone leaf inset and made a note in her day book before they searched the area for more clues.

'Meg never mentioned to you she'd lost an earring, did she, Tim?'

'No, not that I can remember. We'll have to get the police team to check the area for anything connected to Patty and Michael as well.'

'Yes, but first we'd better get these items tested. I'd like to concentrate on Meg at present, so we can eliminate her from our investigation—she is so stressed out by all this.'

Tim grimaced. 'I guess Meg's a suspect now that we have evidence she was at the scene of the crime.'

Sadness clouded Ann's face. 'I hate to say it, but she's the one person here in Auckland with the greatest motive, I'm afraid to say—though if Eddie were here, I'd place my bets on her as a prime suspect.'

They carefully gathered together the exhibits after first taking photos of the exact place where each was found.

'Put them in separate bags and guard them with your life.' Ann shuddered. 'This is beginning to feel rather unnerving to me. I sincerely hope Meg is not implicated in Lyle's murder.'

While Tim carefully removed the twig holding the fabric from the bush and placed it in a sample bag, he looked up to see the downcast look on Ann's face.

'We can't say for sure the earring belongs to Meg—it could be Patty's, or anyone else's for that matter.' He placed it in a separate bag ready to be sent off to the forensic lab.

Ann patted Scout on the head and began walking towards her car. 'I hope you're right—I mean—that it doesn't belong to either of the girls and just a local resident out for a walk.'

As they drove to the police station, Tim was in deep thought.

'You're quiet for a change—something worrying you?' Ann threw him a sideways glance.

'I'm so relieved that Eddie and her daughter won't be harassed by Lyle again.'

When Ann briefly glimpsed at Tim's moist eyes, she gathered that Eddie must have pulled on his heartstrings.

Chapter Thirty-nine

Later that week, Bryce's team at Clovelly Police Station arrested Meg as a possible suspect for Lyle's murder based on circumstantial evidence—although it was still insufficient to charge her. She was remanded on bail at large while the case was under investigation. Ann was gutted she couldn't prevent it.

Meg was relieved they didn't hold her in custody. Her bail conditions involved reporting to the Police Station daily and she could only use her car to drive between Cockle Cove village and home with a GPS tracking monitor.

***

Ann sat next to Tim in a room with a table and chairs at Cockle Cove Police Station. They'd received reports of the forensic samples they'd gathered from Meg, Patty, and Michael earlier in the week.

Ann passed them to Tim and shook her head. 'I think we're barking up the wrong tree. We've missed something.'

Tim perused the documents while his face matched Ann's frown. 'There's nothing matching any of our Persons of Interest except for Meg, unfortunately. That evidence makes her a prime suspect because she was the only one at the scene of the crime. The greenstone earring did belong to her and it matches the DNA on her skirt fibres and hair.'

Ann craned her neck, looking over his shoulder. Her eyes scanned the forensic test results.

Tim continued. 'Look at page three.' He flipped the pages. 'James made a note that if the blunt force trauma on Lyle's abdomen had been inflicted by the handle of Meg's spade, it would have left an impression on his body. But the only marks visible on his abdomen so far, resemble a knuckle imprint.'

'From a thump in the belly,' Ann blurted. 'It's hard to believe that Meg could have inflicted a blow hard enough to leave a pattern from her fist.'

'I agree—I can't see her as a cold-blooded killer either—I really can't.'

Tim's eyes fell on his partner, sitting with her head in her hands, making it obvious she had a soft spot for Meg.

Ann stiffened and sat up. 'To be honest—none of the evidence points to her actually killing Lyle, does it? That only confirms that she was at the crime scene at some point on the evening he was killed. She was digging up a plant, which is not incriminating.'

Tim gazed at Ann, marking her every move as his eyes narrowed.

'Tell the jury that. Unless we can track down someone else at the scene who had just as strong a motive for eliminating Lyle, her chances are slim. She had the motive, and we have evidence she was Johnny-on-the-spot—if you excuse the expression.'

Ann's face fell again. She knew what Tim had said was right but couldn't bear facing it. As if the poor girl hadn't been through enough trauma already.

'Don't you worry, Aunty, we won't give up until we find his killer. If you passionately believe Meg couldn't have done it, we'll get the fiend.'

That's what Ann loved about Tim—the way he could lift her spirits when she was about to give up.

'We'd better move before Meg goes to trial. Time is of the essence now.'

***

Michael had agreed to go into Cockle Cove Police Station to be interviewed rather than at his workplace—as walls have ears, Ann told him—one of her regular sayings.

While he was waiting for his lawyer to arrive before Bryce interviewed him, Ann and Tim sat in a side room in case they were needed during the interview.

Ann picked at her fingernails. 'I'd be interested to hear what he has for an alibi. We have to accept that although we may not find any incriminating evidence on a person that connects them to a homicide, they can still be convicted on circumstantial evidence.'

Tim doodled on a page in his notebook. 'Yeah, and that makes me all the more determined to find the real killer, so the wrong person won't be thrown into prison for life.'

Ann crossed her arms and leaned on the table. 'So, what do you think about Michael—I mean—do you think he is capable of pushing Lyle over the cliff?'

Tim rested his chin in his palm. 'I just don't think he would have as strong a motive as the

255

two women. But the way I'm thinking, if it's possible to convict someone on circumstantial evidence only and we have no direct proof, then it's possible that the killer could have been someone other than the people we have already interviewed.'

Ann knew exactly what Tim said was the one thing that always made crime investigations frustratingly complicated and tedious.

There was a knock at the door, and Bryce's head appeared.

'I'll start Michael's interview shortly. But some other information regarding this case has come to light.'

Ann looked at him—adrenaline shooting through her veins with excited expectation that perhaps they could now follow a new line of enquiry, as her patience was wearing thin.

'One of Patty Gregg's neighbours has contacted the Crime Stop Line with information regarding the homicide of Lyle Doyle.'

Tim stopped his doodling. 'What kind of information?'

Bryce entered the room and sat at the table. 'A woman phoned to say—on the night in question—both she and her husband heard voices outside their home which is located almost adjacent to the crime scene.'

'Did they see who they were?' asked Ann.

'No—a tall, thick hedge surrounds their property. The woman said she couldn't decipher whether a man was shouting at another male or a female.'

Tim was busy making notes. 'But could she understand what they said?'

Bryce shook his head. No, the altercation only lasted a short time—perhaps five minutes—then there was silence. The witness never gave it another thought until she heard the police appealing for public assistance regarding Lyle's death.'

Tim crossed his arms over his chest. 'So, where do we go from here?'

'We wait until I've interviewed Michael Gregg to see if he has an alibi for that evening.'

Ann stood up, shoved her hands inside her coat pockets and began pacing the floor. 'Patty hasn't one either. We need an eyewitness.'

Bryce opened another file he'd carried into the room. 'The constable who found Lyle's Ute parked at the end of the street by the first entrance to the walkway said the crew had interviewed several neighbours but needed to return to visit those who were not at home at the time. That is happening this week.'

The DI left and proceeded to the next room to conduct his interview with Michael Gregg, while Ann and Tim wandered off to the police canteen for a coffee on standby in case Bryce needed them further.

Half an hour later, the DI ducked into the café to see them.

'Sorry, it took longer than I expected. Not much of an alibi, either—no better than the two women. Join me in my office if you don't mind.'

Ann felt frustrated hanging around the station for so long and wanted to get on her way. They followed Bryce into his office and sat down.

'Michael is saying that he left his house in Brightside at approximately five-thirty—a twenty-minute drive to Clovelly Heights to join Patty and Meg for dinner. He reckons his neighbours, the Watsons, can confirm that, as he had been mowing the lawns and spoke to them at his letterbox. He told them he was going inside to take a shower before heading off to have dinner at his daughter's home. Before he drove out of the driveway, they waved at him when he left to visit Patty that evening.'

Ann gave a sceptic grunt. 'Humph—he could have concocted a false alibi in advance.'

Tim was also unconvinced. 'Did they see or hear him return that night?'

'Mrs Watson, the witness, thought she'd heard his garage door not long before midnight, and his security light flashed through their curtains briefly.'

Ann scoffed. 'I guess that isn't entirely a watertight alibi, as he still had time to duck into the Reserve and accost Lyle if he'd seen his Ute on the street.'

Bryce flicked through his report. 'Yes, but we have no incriminating evidence to prove that. No one has come forward to say they saw either him or his car that evening. And the two women don't have witnesses for their alibis for the time of the crime.'

Ann stopped writing, tapping her pen on her notebook. 'I guess we have to keep looking.'

'I think we should focus on the Ute being parked at the entrance to the walkway and question the neighbours again to see if they noticed anything else unusual that evening.'

'I agree with you, Tim. Let's start this afternoon and do a few streets, even if it takes the rest of the week. Someone must have seen something.'

'Okay, Ann.' Bryce stood, pushing his chair back under his desk. 'You two go ahead, and meanwhile I'd better bring Eddie Thorpe's father in for questioning—although it's a long shot.' He closed the file and walked towards the door as the other two detectives made their way to the car park.

Ann took her car keys out of her pocket. 'Come on, Tim—we'll head out after I've had a bit of lunch. 'There's something else I need to do first. Meet me at my house around two.'

Chapter Forty

Meg was thrilled to see Ann and welcomed her with open arms.

'I've got a friend in the car who wants to see Podge.' Ann fastened Scout's lead and locked her car while Meg stood beaming on the doorstep, holding onto her dog's collar.

'Let's see if they remember each other. They must do if they're from the same litter.'

Ann carefully introduced Scout to the Beagle in the doorway. The two women stood smiling as the dogs licked each other, wagging their tails and making happy sounds.

'Come onto the deck. I've made a bit of lunch—just a few filled rolls and a date loaf.'

'Sounds lovely—you always go to a lot of trouble. Thank you.'

Ann unleashed Scout, so the dogs could play together on the gated veranda. Meg brought out the food on a tray with coffee. She knew Ann was a caffeine addict.

After much small talk about dogs, Meg asked Ann if she would like to take their charges for a walk along the bush path behind her house that led to a large pond.

'Sure, I'd love to—I need the exercise.'

Keeping both animals on their leads, they headed along the forest path where Ann relished the cool air after sitting all morning and driving her car. The earthy smell emanating from the fragrant native trees heightened her senses, reminding her of the bush walks she used to take with Terry when he was alive.

Meg didn't appear to be someone who was a murder suspect. 'I just love the bush, don't you?'

Is she in denial? Ann wondered.

'Meg, I wanted this opportunity to question you about your presence at the crime scene, as Tim and I will have to give evidence at your trial.'

Fear crossed Meg's face as its former glow suddenly disappeared.

'Why—I've already made a statement.'

'We found an earring which matches the DNA on your skirt and your hair. You never said you lost it that day.'

Meg went quiet and continued walking.

'Why didn't you tell us?'

'I'm trying to think. What earring was that?'

'Silver with greenstone—a beautiful piece of jewellery.' Ann held up an image on her phone.

'Oh, that one! I'm sorry, I couldn't remember. I thought I'd sucked it up in the vacuum cleaner. I don't remember wearing it that day.'

'Before I leave, I'll need the other earring as evidence for Forensics, sorry.'

Meg shrugged. 'That's okay, as long as it's going to help my case.'

Ann couldn't grasp what she meant by that, as it would most likely have the reverse effect.

'I need you to tell me, why your earring was found at the crime scene—a long distance from where you had dug up the Agapanthus? That plant was near the end of the track by Patty's house, but the crime scene is at the opposite end of the pathway by the first entrance to the Reserve.'

'I'm trying to remember and honestly don't know. That evening is a kind of blur, right now.'

Ann saw the telltale signs of mental stress showing on her face. Deep furrows that weren't there a few weeks ago had formed, just like the dark rings around her eyes.

Ann didn't push her for more information— waiting, hoping Meg might have a moment of lucidness.

'Ah, here we are at the pond, or rather the lake. It's gorgeous, isn't it? So peaceful—I love coming here.' Meg sat on a log and stared at the water, while Ann despaired about how to kick-start Meg's memory bank.

Butterflies of various colours flew under Ann's nose. She followed them to a clump of large shrubs next to the pond, and suddenly had an idea.

'Come and look at this,' she called out to Meg, waving her hand at her.

Ann pointed to the butterflies that covered the shrub. 'Remember what these represent?'

'Yes ... that's me ... set free. I'm one of those butterflies.'

Ann observed her as she stood in deep thought, watching the beautiful creatures hovering overhead and on the plant.

'They remind me of the times I watched them on my special butterfly bush and the day I broke the jar that Lyle used to torture them—and when I let my beautiful blue butterfly go free.' She shuddered and then continued. 'Then all that time I thought I'd pushed Lyle into the sea to drown him.'

Ann leaned on her every word, trying to see where Meg was heading and hoping her plan to unlock her memory was working. It was apparent that her amnesia still troubled her.

'That's how I've been feeling—as though I killed Lyle again. Just as I thought I'd pushed him off the rocks that day and drowned him, my mind plays tricks and tells me I must have pushed him over that cliff in Clovelly.'

'But you didn't, did you?'

Meg broke down, blurting out that she didn't do it. She could remember a few events of that day, but because of the stress of the intense police interview, she kept having memory lapses.

Ann took her arm. 'Let's sit down again on that log over there.'

Meg felt she could trust Ann and opened up. 'I recall wanting to see if there were more Agapanthus plants growing wild further down the track as Patty had said, so I left the first one sitting next to the hole and walked along the track searching for others.'

'Did you dig up any on the way?'

Meg cleared her throat. 'No, but I did see a suitable one near the far end of the track and started digging it up. When I looked around the area, I realised it was within viewing distance of one of the houses and didn't want to cause any trouble, so I put back the soil and left it. I wandered back along the walkway, picked up the plant I had already dug up and carried it with the spade and gloves to my vehicle and drove home.'

Ann dived into her notebook for a minute. 'We have an eyewitness who saw you carrying that plant out to your car—around eight thirty.'

'Yes, I put the Agapanthus and gardening stuff in the car and went home. I promise you I did not see Lyle!'

So there it was, Ann thought. Meg had secured her alibi after revealing she had been in the location of the crime scene with the intention of digging up another Agapanthus—despite having changed her mind—and walked back to her car. That's how her earring ended up there.

Once again, Ann was certain Bryce's team had arrested the wrong person, but she had to follow protocol in this instance. Regardless, she was going to prove them wrong, no matter what.

Chapter Forty-one

Following her lunch visit with Meg, Ann set out with Tim to visit the residents who lived in the streets near the crime scene. She received a call from Bryce who informed her that his superintendent had the forensic evidence re-examined upon the suggestion of James, the Pathologist.

'Since Lyle's death, a significant mark has manifested itself on the victim's skin and underlying tissues that could be a probable match—the imprint on the handle of the spade Meg used near the crime scene.' Bryce hesitated for a second. 'I'm sorry, but my team has just taken her into custody to remain until her trial, and her dog is with a neighbour.'

Ann was both gob-smacked and angry, hanging up on Bryce abruptly. Why hadn't they taken onboard her comments after visiting Meg at her home? She came off the phone shaking.

'Are you alright, Aunty—what's happened? You look like death warmed up.'

'It was Bryce. You wouldn't believe what he said.'

Ann struggled over to a low, white-washed wall at a house on the corner of the street and sat down.

'His superintendent has brought Meg into custody as a prime suspect, as they have found further evidence connecting her to Lyle's death.'

'What? That can't be. There must be some mistake!'

Ann leaned forward over her knees, telling Tim about the re-examination of evidence following the discovery of bruising and imprints on Lyle's body.

'I'll have to get to see her and offer support. She won't survive incarceration. Her neighbour, a dog lover, is caring for Podge. But I think I should offer to take him, as he'll be company for Scout. Perhaps I can mention it when I see her in the remand cells.'

Tim couldn't think of anything to say that could remove the look of defeat on Ann's face.

'I know she'll appreciate that—your offer of support, I mean.'

Ann jumped to her feet. 'Let's get this show on the road first and see if we can find the real culprit. As I said, Meg is no killer.'

Door knocking wasn't up Ann's alley. But she knew this could be a sure way of getting results. Sometimes a neighbour remembers something they didn't recall at first. Often all members of a household are not interviewed at the time the police officers are in the area. It was always prudent to revisit homes located near the crime scene. That was Ann's motto.

'Tim—let's first concentrate on the side streets, as officers have already been up and down the main road that runs parallel with the cliff walkway. We can do one side at a time.' Ann repositioned her sunhat and took another mouthful of water from the pump bottle she carried.

They first focused their attention on a short cul-de-sac directly opposite the entrance to the walkway that opened within metres of the crime scene. There were not more than twenty homes.

After enquiring whether the residents had seen any unusual activity that evening, they came to a standstill. Nothing!

Ann sat on a park bench at the entrance to the Reserve where several homes bordered the cliff edge.

'Absolutely nix to report. How about you, Tim?' She took another few mouthfuls of water.

'The same. Some of them didn't even have a clue that a homicide had taken place metres from their homes. Unbelievable!'

Ann removed her hat and ran her fingers through her hair. 'Thank God it's a bit cooler today. This is the more frustrating side of detective work, as you are finding out.'

Her phone rang. This time it was Meg's sister, Angela, in a frantic state.

'What have they done to Meg?' Angela blurted down the phone. 'She has had a complete melt down in that cell. I thought she was supposed to be out on Remand at large?'

Ann turned on her speaker so Tim could hear. 'I'm so sorry, Angela—she was—but Forensics has produced new evidence that connects her to the assault on Lyle.'

Ann furtively checked around her that no one else was listening and turned off her speaker phone just in case, while Tim tried to follow her conversation.

'What kind of state?'

Angela ranted about Meg having one of the worst attacks of amnesia that she'd ever witnessed, probably due to the excessive emotional stress of being locked up.

Ann ground her teeth and then rubbed her jaw.

'She doesn't even recognise me!' Angela shouted down the phone. 'You've got to get her out of this situation before it kills her!'

'I promise I'll talk to one of the chiefs at the CIB and see what we can do.'

'You need to show the Defence lawyers the file with her Neurologist's report. It describes the long-term effects of the head injury caused by the heavy blow she'd sustained from Lyle.'

'Yes, I'll do that. We have the file and were going to use it for the Police Prosecution at Lyle's trial for GBH.'

Angela's voice shook. 'You need to visit her as soon as you can and see for yourself. She doesn't know why they locked her up—I mean, Meg doesn't even remember being a suspect for Lyle's death.'

'I'll go there today and show Detective Inspector Drummond that report. I promise I'll push to get her out somehow.'

Angela slammed the phone down in her ear. But being a seasoned detective, Ann knew people react irrationally in these situations, and poor Angela had a good reason for exploding.

Chapter Forty-two

When Ann finished her call, Tim pointed along the road. 'Shall we move on and do the rest of the side streets?'

Ann wiped her brow. 'Yes, sure, but let me draw breath if you don't mind.'

He gave her a half-smile and kept his mouth shut

A few minutes later, Ann picked up her document satchel and water bottle before traipsing after Tim along Clovelly Road to the next side street.

This road had a lot more homes and would take much longer to visit each resident. But Ann was determined she would not miss anyone—that vital eyewitness who was going to keep Meg out of prison. For at this point of the investigation, she was still a key suspect who had been in the area close to the time of Lyle's death and had a strong motive to erase him. But in Ann's eyes, it was unlikely she committed the offence.

'You take this side of the street and I'll do the other. Remember—if anyone can give us a clue, let me know and I'll question them too.'

After Ann said that, she wanted to take it back—worried that Tim would think she didn't trust his judgement.

'Oh, and you do the same with me, okay?' she added.

'Right you are, Aunty, I'll get onto it.'

Although Tim was a junior partner, it was Ann who had a wealth of experience, and although she never said it to Tim, he still had a great deal to learn. She'd built up this business on her own and also had a notable reputation—something that had to be earned through years of doing the hard yards.

Ann was wondering where they would head next in this investigation if the house enquiries led to a blind alley. Until now, everything they had gathered for this case was circumstantial. They didn't really have a suspect—only people with motive who had acted suspiciously—which accounted for nothing without being able to prove any of them guilty beyond reasonable doubt. In this country, everyone is innocent until proven guilty.

Ann's throat was dry. She'd asked one of the residents in the street to top up her drink bottle, and the woman also asked if she would like a cup of tea. In fact, up until now, Ann had received multiple offers but had declined each one, as time was of an essence. She didn't want some over-enthusiastic police officer in Bryce's team rushing out and arresting anyone else in haste, just because they couldn't find a prime suspect and evidence to prove it.

Hot and tired—every ounce of flesh of this detective's body was calling out for mercy, wanting to pack it in and go home. Her voice had become hoarse, and she abhorred the repetition of it all, but pushed on.

The phone's vibration in her pocket startled Ann, as she was about to enter another resident's gate.

It was Tim. 'We're in luck—I've found a reliable witness who saw Lyle park at the end of the street near the first entrance to the Reserve and another car hovering around the area as well. Can you come to number five? I'm further down the street than you are.'

Ann felt her heart race. In fact, she experienced uncomfortable palpitations when excited, and right now she was ecstatic. Turning to walk along the street, she clutched her chest and looked for number five, then spotted Tim standing at the letterbox.

'Are you alright, Aunty? You look as though you're having a heart attack!'

Ann stopped, clutching her chest. 'I'm fine, I've just had a few palpitations—you know—the ones I often get when I'm excited. Now, tell me the gist before we go inside.'

'The witness said he was on his way home and saw the white Ute park on the street, and the driver go down to the Reserve walkway. A blue Honda from Opus Rental caught his eye as it coasted past the parked vehicle. It hesitated as if the driver was looking for the owner and then he turned the car into this street, parking on the corner outside the house there.'

'Okay, I'll go in and see what else he can tell us.'

Just as the detectives had finished talking outside by the front steps, the witness opened the door and invited Tim back inside with Ann in tow.

After flashing her ID, Ann began to question him. 'When the rental paused next to the white Ute, did you see anyone else on the street?'

'Nobody—it was like a ghost town. I've never seen anyone park on that side before, as there isn't much space for vehicles. They usually stop in the Reserve car park further down Clovelly Road to preserve the privacy of the residents next to the walkway.'

Ann was busy jotting everything down while Tim peered through the man's blinds.

'You have full view of the spot where the Honda was parked. Did you notice what time the vehicle moved off, or did you see the driver?' asked Tim.

'I poked my head out the window and saw a man racing to that car around ten—or thereabouts. It was dark, but I could tell he was agitated, as he sped off like Zorro.'

'Did you take down the vehicle registration of either cars?'

'No, I honestly didn't think there was a need for that. Not until he drove off in a hurry. Why— has he done something bad? You don't think he's the ... killer ... involved with that poor fellow's death, do you?'

'We don't know. But now I want you to try extra hard to think of anything you can remember about the way he dressed or any description of him at all.'

The man went quiet, in deep thought. Ann glanced at Tim, raising her eyebrows, as the witness took longer than expected to answer.

This is our last hope of progressing this case. If he can't help us, we're up the creek without a paddle,' thought Ann.

'I know! I remember being concerned that his vehicle was still there and wondered if perhaps he'd fallen over the cliff after going for a walk in the dark. It has happened before. I kept poking my nose through the blinds to check if he'd returned to his car, and then he appeared—the street light gave me a tiny glimpse of him.'

Ann sat erect in her chair. 'Tell us anything you can remember about his appearance—anything.'

'He was partly bald, as I can remember, with his head shining under the light. The rest is difficult, as the streetlamp was too far back, and I only caught a glimpse. I can barely remember what he wore ... I think he had covered shoes and some kind of jacket and trousers. I couldn't even recall seeing the colour.'

"That's enough for now. We can talk to the rental car company and they'll help with his identity. You've been a great help, and with your consent, we'll use this as evidence. You may be called as an eyewitness once we catch the culprit, but I'll be in touch. Thank you so much for helping us with our investigation.'

Chapter Forty-three

Ann dropped Tim home to write up reports from the evidence they'd gathered from their door-knocking sessions. After arriving at the police station, she headed straight for the remand cells to visit Meg. She had arranged to meet with Bryce later to discuss Meg's detainment and also about bringing in Jonathan for questioning.

It was difficult for Ann to look at the forlorn shadow of a woman who was in a much different state to the one she'd lunched with earlier that day. Perhaps all hope Meg had of thwarting police suspicions of her killing her *so-called* husband in cold blood was gone.

But Meg didn't know that Ann had no power to stop that. The CIB team was in charge of the homicide now.

'I guess you've been told that Forensics found an imprint on Lyle's abdomen from blunt trauma. It appears to match the pattern from a stamp on the metal handle of your spade. It isn't a hundred percent confirmed, but it is highly probable, they said.'

Meg glared at her. 'I don't know what you're talking about—what spade? And what's all this about trauma to Lyle's abdomen?'

Meg clutched either side of her temples and began to massage them. 'I didn't push him in the sea with the spade. I can vaguely recall him slipping off a rock but can't remember what happened after that. He didn't come home that evening. Sorry—it's just that now and then my memory plays tricks on me and I imagine I have done something wrong.'

'I understand. It must be extremely confusing for you.'

'Ask Angela—she'll tell you what happened when Lyle went fishing.'

Ann took a deep breath and let it out, trying not to sigh. This was a tricky situation, but she believed Meg was having a proper amnesia attack.

'Meg—it's not about the time Lyle fell off the rock into the water. Can you remember when Tim and I told you he had fallen off the cliff and died?'

Meg sat on the bed staring directly ahead, obviously trying hard to remember.

'I can recall when you told me the news that he was dead, but I can't remember the rest of the details. Did I kill him?'

'I don't think so, but it appears that someone pushed him off the cliff in Clovelly Reserve after whacking him with a blunt instrument. The forensic team seems to think you may have rammed the metal handle of your spade into his stomach forcing him over the precipice.'

Whirlpools of fear swirled in the whites of Meg's eyes. 'What? Why would I have been there?'

'You don't remember digging up Agapanthus plants the evening you had dinner with Patty and her father?'

Meg sat twirling her hair repeatedly around her finger. 'I remember gardening with Patty, and she gave me an Agapanthus.'

'Think about that evening and try to recall your steps. It'll be easier for you to do that here with me than in a courtroom harassed by ruthless Prosecutors.'

Rivers of tears began to gush down Meg's flushed cheeks. Ann passed her a white handkerchief from her jacket pocket. 'Here—it's clean. I always keep a spare for situations like this. She gave her a warm smile.

'Why am I going through hell again—and when will it come to an end? I haven't done anything wrong,' Meg snivelled.

Ann walked over and sat on the cell bed, placing a hand on her arm. 'I know it has been a nightmare for you. That's why it's important to have a good recollection of what you did the night of Patty's dinner party and your gardening spree with her, planting roses. Think back to when you were about to leave to drive home.'

Meg thought hard. 'That evening there was a lovely full moon, and I wanted to go for a walk in the Reserve. At first, Michael and Patty thought they might come with me after our meal had gone down, but later they were too tired, and I left to go home.'

'That's it, Meg. See—you can remember. Just take it slowly.' Ann squeezed her arm.

'I was annoyed, as I guessed Patty was just hanging around waiting to see Lyle and get into conflict with him over changing her witness statement. She told me she'd take great delight in telling him she'd never do that but wished to say it to his face.'

'And you—didn't you want to say something to him?'

'I was told it would harm the case if I was caught fraternising with the accused before his trial.'

'It was hardly fraternising. And if he was at Patty's house while you were there, that doesn't make you guilty of breaking the law—does it?'

Meg shrugged. 'I guess so.'

'Did anyone go on the walk with you?'

'I can't remember—oh wait—no. I recall standing on the walkway alone, looking at the moon and wondering if there was any life up there.'

Ann could see that Meg was fading—probably emotionally exhausted—but she didn't want to lose her testimony now that they were so close.

'Can I get you a glass of water?'

'Yes, please. I'm parched.'

Ann stuck her head out the door and asked the constable to fetch it. He brought back a glass with a jug, placed it on a side table then left.

'Carry on ... where was I ... oh, yes. Did you see anyone else in the Reserve that evening—anyone at all?'

Meg shook her head. 'Nope, not a soul—and I was beginning to get the creeps. I stood wondering how on earth I got there.'

'What do you mean—whether you drove or walked there?'

Ann carefully observed Meg's body language and could see she was trying hard to remember and did not believe for a minute that she was pretending.

'No—I mean—one minute I was sitting having supper with Patty before I left her house to go home and the next I recall her waving at me as I pulled out of her driveway.'

'Yes, she has verified that. Where did you go after you drove off?'

'That's just it—I can't recollect anything else except standing under the bright light of a full moon staring out at the sea, mesmerised by the moonbeams on the white crests of the waves. A shudder went through me when I realised I was standing in an empty Reserve on my own late at night.'

That must have been after she'd put the plant and spade in her car and walked to the other end of the reserve near the crime scene, thought Ann.

The detective was frustrated that this testimony was quite different to the statement Meg had initially given when first interviewed.

'What did you do then—try to think back? Your freedom could depend on it.'

As soon as Ann said this, she called to mind something Angela had said. She'd described how pressure and stress could heighten Meg's amnesia condition.

Ann stroked her hand. 'Take your time, Meg—it's going to be alright. Just tell me, as you recall that night.'

'That's just it—I can't. My mind goes blank when I remember the moon and how beautiful the sea looked. I suddenly felt vulnerable and went home.'

Ann realised she couldn't push the fragile woman any more—it was time to let her rest.

She was eager to go back home and type up her notes, before talking to Bryce about Meg's neurologist's report.

'So—can I leave? I don't know why I should be here, and I need to get back to Podge.'

'Your dog is fine—he's with your neighbour, Peggy, until you get home.'

'But I haven't done anything wrong. Can't you do anything?'

'I'm sorry—don't despair.' Ann felt like a fraud, with no words of hope to comfort her.

Meg began to sob. 'I can't bear the thought of spending the rest of my life in prison. I was incarcerated all my married life! I thought I was free now. Please, Ann, you've got to make them believe me.'

Ann said what she could to pacify her and promised to take good care of Podge if she remained in custody. But now the pressure really was on her to solve this case and find the real killer, as she was still convinced it wasn't Meg.

Chapter Forty-four

Desperate to get away from it all, Ann needed a short break before returning to the station. It had been some time since she'd visited the Leisure Centre gym for a workout, but now the rot had begun in and her joints were stiff—a symptom of sitting around too much and driving her car everywhere.

She was surprised to see fewer vehicles in the carpark than usual. After doing the circuit on the machines, she headed for the swimming pool, which was the main attraction of the Leisure Centre, as far as she was concerned.

While completing her last lap of breaststroke in the pool, her mind kept struggling with the upsetting image of Eddie's father, Jonathan, behind bars. Could he have done it? The only proof they had from the eyewitness was the rental car he drove. The man who saw him could hardly describe the driver accurately. But now they had confirmation from the Opus Rental people that it was definitely Jonathan who drove the car that night, as it was the only blue Honda sedan in the fleet.

Ann could have stayed in the pool for longer, but she knew Bryce had arranged to discuss Jonathan's interview with them after he finished with him. She slipped under a hot shower, relishing the soothing water pounding on the back of her neck, until becoming aware that once again, she was in the thick of a complicated crime mystery.

Since Ann had left the police force as a highly respected Detective Inspector, none of her criminal cases had been easy to solve. Although not intentionally setting out to handle homicides initially, how did she always end up in these situations? What she was meant to be doing as a part-time private detective, was tracking unfaithful spouses, petty thieves and unruly teenagers. So much for semi-retirement.

While dressing, she received a text from Tim. He was waiting for her at the police station, as Bryce had notified him that he'd completed Jonathan's interview.

'Oh, blast, time for a holiday,' Ann mumbled, as she stuffed her swimming things into her gym bag and trudged out to her Land Rover ready to hear Bryce's verdict.

As she drove to the station, she thought of Jonathan's family in Brisbane—Eddie and Sophie waiting for the child's grandfather to return home. And Eddie thinking he had just gone to Auckland to attend Lyle's trial as a witness for Meg. A shudder went through her as she said a wee prayer for Jonathan and his loved ones—that he wouldn't be charged with murder.

Bryce greeted Ann in the foyer of the station. 'Come into my office. Tim is waiting for you there. I've just finished questioning Jonathan Thorpe.'

'Has he been released?'

'No, he's still in the interview room. I thought you and Tim may want to interrogate him following your eyewitness's statement. He has confessed to be the person in the rental car by the Reserve that evening.'

Ann wanted to talk it over with Bryce first. As they both entered his office, Bryce said, 'Tim— how about grabbing a couple of coffees for us before the canteen closes—if you don't mind.'

Tim looked up from his iPad and gave Bryce a disapproving glare, as if to insinuate that he wasn't his boss. Ann observed his body language and nodded at him winking before he walked off to get the coffees.

'It's not looking good for Jonathan, as he has no alibi whatsoever for being in the Reserve at that late hour,' said Bryce. 'I remember you telling me Patty had spoken to Eddie about Lyle breaching his bail, saying he was going to drop by and see her that night. Jonathon knew he was going to be in the area.'

Tim brought the coffees on a cardboard tray and placed them on Bryce's desk.

'Well done! We were waiting for you to come before I discussed the interview.'

Ann felt that Bryce was somewhat patronising of Tim and not entirely honest, as he had discussed the case before her partner had arrived through the door. A hint of competitiveness, perhaps. *What's all that about?* She wondered.

He reiterated what he'd told Ann.

'So, what was his alibi?' Tim asked Bryce with a frown.

'He said he only wanted to protect Patty from Lyle, which is hard to believe, as she would have told Eddie her father was coming to meet Meg and stay for dinner. Isn't that what you told us after you spoke on the phone to Eddie?'

'That's right, but he may have still wanted to talk to Lyle and warn him off.'

Ann became agitated. 'Now, wait on—get straight to the point. Did Jonathan admit to seeing Lyle that evening at all?'

'No, and he wouldn't discuss it. That's why I'm holding him on remand as a suspect.'

Tim stood erect. 'I should have been in the interview. I got to know Eddie really well in Brisbane. Perhaps I could try talking to him about her and Sophie to soften him up.'

Bryce mellowed. 'Well, of course, that's why I've brought you here. You can tell him you have an eyewitness who saw him getting into the car and that we can arrest him on that.'

Ann stood up. 'We'll work on him—leave him to us.'

She was eager to move on to the interview room and make progress—annoyed that Bryce had insisted that he interview Jonathan in the first instant, as though he didn't want to let go of the reins. Ann was also upset that the DI didn't give Tim the credit he deserved, for in her eyes, her partner was a top-notch detective in every way, even without the years of experience behind him. Perhaps Bryce wanted her all to himself, seeing they were such close friends.

'Now that's a thought', she muttered softly to herself.

Bryce leaned back on his chair, folding his arms. 'His lawyer is with him, keeping a tight rein—just warning you. I'll talk to you later.'

Chapter Forty-five

Jonathan flashed his eyes around the room, avoiding Ann's gaze as she sat flicking the end of her pen and then stopped, aware it was probably unnerving him. She was waiting for Tim to finish perusing the notes in his file, as she'd asked him to talk to Jonathan about Eddie and Sophie.

Tim commenced—eyeballing Jonathan.

'I know why you came here—initially—I mean. It wasn't only to give testimony at Lyle's trial, was it?'

Ann's eyes focused on the suspect's body language, rather than what he said, while Tim weighed heavily on his every word.

Jonathan's lawyer, Hamish, leaned over and whispered in his client's ear who cast his eyes downward. 'No comment.'

Tim continued. 'But I know you came here to protect two precious people in your life—your eldest daughter and granddaughter.'

Again, he made no comment after his lawyer whispered in his ear.

After playing cat and mouse for a good half hour, Jonathan became uncomfortable. He knew he was getting the detectives' backs up, and they were infuriated at his making *no comment* responses when questioned. But when Bryce entered the room and began interrogating him, he began to cower.

The DI took over. 'The blue Honda from Opus Rental you had hired was seen parked in a side street opposite the Reserve. What were you doing there at that time?'

Jonathan suddenly found his tongue. 'I couldn't sleep worrying about the trial and the room was stuffy. It was a humid evening, so decided to go for a drive.'

Bryce's face adopted an expression as stern as his voice. 'What a coincidence you chose to go to the very spot where Lyle Doyle had parked his Ute that evening. I think you need to tell me exactly what you were doing there.'

Jonathan took out a crumpled handkerchief and blew his nose loudly, while Ann's mouth curved as she detected fear in the man's eyes.

'I couldn't sleep worrying about my daughter Eddie, and granddaughter, Sophie. What if that monster was set free again? He would torment my girls for the rest of their lives.'

Bryce's eyes became slits as he pushed his face into Jonathan's who sat pulling at his fingers, almost dislocating his knuckles.

Tim's eyes fixated on a large signet ring on Jonathan's right hand. He scribbled a note and handed it to Ann. She nodded in agreement.

'And what did you do that night to alleviate your anxiety? I can understand you wanting to get rid of this man.'

Hamish whispered in his ear again.

'I wasn't trying to get rid of him—I only wanted to talk.'

'Threaten him, you mean,' Bryce growled.

By this time, Tim felt sorry for Jonathan. He still had a soft spot for Eddie and had promised to try to keep her father out of trouble. But was it too late?

Hamish asked the detectives to let him speak to his client alone. When they returned to the interview room, Jonathan's tone had changed. He was now willing to speak about what had happened the night of Lyle's death.

He explained how Patty had told Eddie she was expecting Lyle to arrive sometime that evening but had no idea what time he would turn up. Jonathan was desperate to plea bargain with Lyle—bribe him with a ton of money to stay away from his family and never go near them again, but Lyle refused.

'It was an ownership thing,' he muttered. 'Lyle saw women as trophies he collected—and my granddaughter, or his child, was something he had created. He'd managed to contact and threaten Eddie, saying he would take Sophie far away from her. It's his narcissism and not love that made him feel entitled.'

Ann's heart melted as Jonathan continued his story.

'I found out where he lived, as I saw him in the village. Eddie had given me his car licence number, so I followed him. I was waiting until I could get him on his own somewhere to talk, but it never happened.'

The listeners watched Jonathon struggling to keep his composure in the face of Bryce's continued brisk questioning.

'Carry on.'

'When Eddie told me that Lyle would be visiting Patty—trying to get her to change her witness statement—I grabbed the chance to confront him.'

Ann looked him in the eye. 'So, you carried no weapon of any kind?'

'No, I only wanted to warn him off my girls, like I said.'

Ann could see a flush of red making its way up Jonathan's neck. He looked around.

'Can I have another glass of water, please?'

Bryce asked a constable to fetch it and carried on his line of questioning. Before long, Jonathan broke down—telling how he'd stalked Lyle and waited for him to drive out to Clovelly Heights.

'After Lyle had parked his Ute on Clovelly Road near the first entrance to the Reserve, I waited until he had got out and watched him walk through the alleyway between the houses and disappear into the night.'

'And that's when you drove into Pelican Drive and parked not far from the corner of Clovelly Road.' Bryce's eyes flashed. 'Our eyewitness watched you get out of your car and head into the Reserve too.'

'It was pretty dark, but there was a full moon. A security light shone brightly from one of the houses behind a tall hedge, and as I hurried, I could see Lyle creeping along the walkway trying to dodge the light, which I did too. About halfway along the path, I caught him up and called his name softly.'

Ann looked up, observing Jonathan as he seemed to be reluctant to continue. He turned to

Hamish and jotted something down on his notepad, showing it to him.

The attorney nodded. 'Yes, go ahead.'

'Lyle swung around, and when I said I was Jonathan, Eddie's father, he went ballistic—raving on about why I was here, deliberately trying to ruin his trial. He ran at me like a wild bull and got me in a headlock. I managed to twist my way out of it and then tried to talk to him sensibly.'

'Is this when you pushed him over the edge of the cliff?' Bryce pushed his face forward at him with raised eyebrows.

'No! I offered him a hundred-thousand dollars if he agreed to stay out of my girls' lives. I did not throw him over the edge, as you describe it. Lyle punched me in the guts with his fist and then used a Judo movement to hurl me onto the ground. I honestly thought he was going to shove me down that precipice. I was able to keep away from the edge while still trying to reason with him, but he was in a towering rage and kicked me in the back. Before he got really stuck into me, I managed to get back on my feet, and then he lunged at me again.'

Bryce's eyes scrutinised him. 'How did you react, then?'

'I've also done Martial Arts over the years, but he was much stronger, and his anger added to that strength. I punched him hard in the belly, telling him never to go near my girls again or I would finish him. It was never my intention to kill him. I threatened to go public about his abuse of women and said I would completely end his business career.'

Ann looked him in the eye. 'Did you kill him?'

'No, I didn't even think about pushing him off the cliff—I just meant to give him a good hiding and get a promise from him to leave my girls alone. As I said before—he was so much stronger than me that I sort of gave up. When I turned to go back to my car, he was standing still, but then as I moved away he acted drunk-like and couldn't walk straight. He must have turned and wandered off in the wrong direction and stumbled over the edge.'

Ann clasped her hands across her chest. 'I see. So, you are saying you acted in self-defence.'

'That's right. If I hadn't reacted the way I did, I wouldn't be here to tell the story and my girls would have lost a loving father and granddad.'

Ann continued. 'What happened then?'

'Before I exited the walkway, I glanced over my shoulder and he was gone—no sign of him. I hesitated, shining the light from my cell phone down the walkway and could see he'd disappeared. I guessed he must have ducked off between the houses. I didn't want to hang around in case he jumped out at me from nowhere.'

Jonathan sat with his head in his hands, trying hard not to blubber. With a muffled voice he kept saying he didn't mean to do it, over and over. He pulled his head up and leaned on the desk—his teary eyes revealing dark hollows underneath.

Bryce stood up. 'You do realise you are now a Prime Suspect in this investigation, and I'll have to charge you with GBH. You'll be held in custody on remand. If the coroner can prove that the punch you gave Doyle caused his fall over the precipice, you could be up for involuntary manslaughter.'

Ann glared at Bryce. 'Wait—can I have a word—alone?'

She left Tim in the room with Jonathan and the lawyer while she and Bryce disappeared into the interview room next door and sat down.

'I want to talk to you before you charge him, please.' Ann tried to calm her breathing.

There was a knock at the door as Tim poked his head in. 'Sorry, guys—do you mind if I have a word too?'

Bryce glanced at Ann for approval.

She smiled warmly and nodded. 'Yes, I'd prefer you to join us, Tim. Take a seat.'

'I was about to say to Bryce that we can avoid charging him with involuntary manslaughter,' said Ann. 'To me it was clearly self-defence. If Lyle had continued to lurch at Jonathan, he would have gone over that precipice instead. That bully was a Judo expert and in a rage, likely unaware of his own strength. Self-defence is what it is.'

'I totally agree,' Tim blurted. 'Eddie was terrified of him returning to Australia and getting shared custody of Sophie—or worse— harming them both. It is apparent he was only defending his family by confronting Lyle. He has denied intending to harm him, and that's how it should stay. There's no evidence to say he intended to kill him.'

Bryce hesitated, rubbing his chin. 'Well, okay—you win—I trust your judgement. I guess we can't charge him with Involuntary Manslaughter without an eyewitness. It'll be difficult to prove. Let's go back and talk to him.'

Tim beckoned the detectives to stop. 'Wait— I think we should send that large signet ring Jonathan wears on his right hand to Forensics. I have an idea that if he wore it when he punched

Lyle, there may be evidence of that on his skin, which would back up his story and exonerate Meg.'

Bryce reached next to him and patted Tim on the back in his usual patronising way, although Tim knew it wasn't ill-intentioned. It was just one of his quirks.

'Good thinking—young man. That brain of yours certainly comes to the party at the last minute. I'll get one of my officers to fetch it off him and send it right away to Forensics.'

Tim's eyes gleamed while Ann threw him an approving glance. 'And what about Meg—can we release her now?'

Bryce tapped his pen on the desk in deep thought. 'I'll inform the Senior Prosecutor. You can tell Meg she is now off the hook as the charges will be dropped and she can go home. I have recommended—in liaison with her sister—that Meg receive counselling for Acute Stress Disorder.'

Ann quietly clapped. 'Great news!'

The DI leaned forward on his desk, clasping his hands. 'The Police Psychiatrist has already been to see her and agreed that she should be allowed to stay with her sister rather than here. Angela has been nominated as Meg's carer until she recovers from this latest trauma.'

Ann's eyes moistened. 'That's exactly what I hoped would happen. The poor girl has been to hell and back—enough to tip anyone over the edge. But she'll come right soon, now that the monster, Lyle, is out of her life for good.'

Bryce smirked. 'Hmm, I'm sure you won't be the only one thinking that. Anyway, let's move on to the task in hand.'

Chapter Forty-six

One month later

Ann sat at her dining table thinking over the events of the past few months. She felt sorry for Jonathan, who had pleaded not guilty to the charge of Involuntary Manslaughter and won his case.

Forensics had successfully matched the imprint of his signet ring to the marks on Lyle's abdomen, which at first the pathologists had thought was from the metal stamp on the handle of Meg's spade. Even though the Defence team were successful in proving that Lyle's demise was a case of self-defence, the Prosecutor had grilled Jonathon until he was almost in tears—extremely emotional because he was also defending his family.

The Defence had argued that if Jonathan hadn't taken the action of fighting back, Lyle would have continued pushing him until he hurtled over the cliff edge. He had already proved himself to be a very violent man, and this Defendant was only rightfully protecting his granddaughter and her mother. The jury returned a unanimous Not Guilty verdict.

A fortnight after the trial, Lyle's body was released by the Coroner for his funeral. The only people who attended were a handful of fishing mates. He had been an only child, whose father was dead, and his mother was too frail to travel so far across the sea. It was a brief and morbid event.

***

Ann stood in her kitchen pondering the past months' events, glad that she could now begin to get her life back on track—really looking forward to a break. She was waiting for Meg and Podge to arrive for some girls' time, and then after lunch they would take both the dogs for a run along the beach.

'Darn!' She reached into the oven and pulled out a rather brown and crisp looking asparagus quiche with parmesan cheese.

Within a short time, Scout ran outside, barking at the gate. His new playmate had arrived, and Meg stepped out of her car looking the best Ann had ever seen her. She wore a dress with colours matching the autumn leaves on the Oak trees in Ann's driveway.

Wow, what a change from the dishevelled frump of a girl I saw when she was in custody, thought Ann. *She looks years younger.*

During lunch, Meg told Ann how she had been like a mother to her—the way she had taken her under the wing and emotionally supported her. 'And guess what,' Meg said—eyes sparkling. 'Jonathan has paid for a return flight for me to go to Brisbane to stay with Eddie for two weeks. I'm over the moon. Would you mind looking after Podge for me?'

'That's wonderful, Meg—of course I'll take care of him. I guess that's Jonathan's way of showing his appreciation for the amazing witness statement you gave in his defence in court—saying thank you for his freedom.'

Ann reflected for a minute on the courageous words Meg had spoken under oath about the brutality she'd received at the hands of her make-believe husband, Lyle.

'You have all escaped his lair. If he were still alive, I'm sure he would have found a way to get off those charges by blackmailing a lawyer.'

Meg lurched forward and hugged her. 'But you never gave up on me—I won't forget.'

'Come on, let's get this lunch eaten—Scout is breaking down the door to take off to the beach.'

After their meal, Meg took off her shoes so she could run like a free spirit and feel the earth under her feet. This time, Ann let Scout off the lead so he could tear off along the beach with Podge and Meg chasing after him—Meg holding her shoes and laughing. It was times like this that Ann knew why she had become a detective—the rewards were great and truly worthwhile. Although this butterfly's wings were still a little crumpled, she was, at last, about to take flight again.

****

At the end of the day, after Meg and Podge had returned home, Ann was worn out. It had been an emotional afternoon and she hoped to take a long break before her next case. She sat at the dining table thinking about what to prepare for her evening meal and just couldn't be bothered. It would have to be a toastie night. Just as she was about to turn on the grill, there was a knock at the door. Not expecting anyone, she walked over to the lounge window and pulled a drape aside. It was Tim, holding a sizeable bunch of flowers.

'Goodness, what brings you here this evening, and what gorgeous flowers? It's not my birthday until next month.'

Tim grinned with amusement. 'I know that, Aunty. I just wanted to say thank you for everything.'

Ann appeared puzzled and invited him into the lounge. 'Have you eaten?'

'Not yet—I wasn't going to stay long. I'm off overseas for a few weeks again.

'Please stay for a bite. I'm about to put cheese toasties under the grill if you'd like to join me. And how about a glass of Guinness?'

'Great, yes I will.'

'So—what are the flowers in aid of?'

'All the amazing support you've given me since I joined Calamity Unlimited. You've been a gem to work with—although I guess the same could not have been said of me. I've learnt so much from you.'

'And the same definitely can be said of you, Tim. You're my rock, and I'm sure Bryce Drummond and his crew quietly think you're going to waste in my employ, when really you should be working for the CIB.'

Tim shook his head. 'No, Aunty. The work we carry out is just as pertinent—or more to the point—far more extensive than what they do. It's just that we wear a different hat.'

Ann knew he was right. 'Now to change the subject—what is this trip overseas? I hope you're coming back.'

Tim chuckled. 'Of course—I'll be back—but I need to pay my parents another visit. They do worry about me in this game, and I like to reassure them.'

Ann gave him a wry smile. She rescued the toasties and pulled them out of her bench top oven using forceps. 'Ow!'

'Are you okay in there?' He rushed to her aid.

'Fine—just singed my finger on the melted cheese.' She held her hand under the cold tap.

'I think there may be someone else who expects you to visit while you're there.'

Tim blushed. 'Yes, you mean Eddie. How did you know?'

Ann beamed at him.

Tim quickly changed the subject. 'Did you hear that the High Court has awarded her damages which have been paid out of Lyle's estate? It is compensation for ruining her life, abandoning his own daughter and avoiding paying child maintenance all those years.'

'It's about time they had a silver lining in the dark cloud hovering over their lives. But what was left of his estate—did she tell you?'

'Eddie wrote and told me that the funds from the sale of Lyle's manufacturing plants in Brisbane and Auckland were still in his company's bank account, which I guess Meg also knew nothing about.'

Ann raised her eyebrows. 'Goodness! Did Eddie and Sophie receive all of that?'

'No. The proceeds from the sale of the factory in Brisbane were granted to Eddie. Meg was awarded the money from the plant in Auckland. The funds were still in Lyle's business account.'

Ann listened open-mouthed. 'So the fiend was loaded.'

'You already know that the court also gave Meg total possession of their matrimonial home because that had been purchased with her inheritance and had been completely under Lyle's control with only his name on the property title.'

Ann placed the toasties in front of him.

'Thanks—these look scrummy.' He nibbled the melted cheese from the side of the toast before he took a bite.

'So what about dear Sophie? She should have been compensated too,' said Ann.

'Eddie has only recently received news that Lyle's company continues to receive royalties from the manufacture of his drones in NZ and Australia. The court has awarded the company to Sophie, as compensation. Of course, Eddie will manage it until Sophie comes of age. As long as the machines continue to be produced, she will receive a regular income from them.'

Ann sat down at the table. 'At last, all his victims have been compensated. Except the kind of damage Lyle has done to a person's spirit, can never really be recompensed.'

'Let's eat and take our minds off the rogue and his ugly shenanigans,' said Tim.

Ann brightened. 'Meg mentioned Jonathan had offered to pay for her, Patty, and you to visit Eddie and Sophie, as you are all connected somehow.'

'You're onto it, Aunty. Patty said she'll come, and Eddie has room for us all, but I'll be staying with my parents.'

'Nice and safe there, aren't you?' Ann winked.

She knew that Tim was not ready to let go of his late sweetheart, Mary, and start dating. But she was also aware he had a soft spot for Eddie.

'That's great—you all getting together over there—sharing your experiences. But remember you can't discuss police business—keep it above board.'

'So, what's on the agenda next when I get back from my trip, Aunty?'

'Just forget about work for a while and go away and have fun. This has been an intense few months and we both need a proper break.'

'How are you going to do that, Aunty? Wouldn't you like to go away somewhere for a decent holiday?'

That would be nice if I had someone to share it with, she thought.

'I'm going to take care of Podge while Meg's away, and I may take the dogs for a few bush walks. Who knows, maybe they'll dig up a body or two up in the Ranges—another case for us to solve.'

'Jeepers! Don't you ever stop thinking about work?'

'It's not really work, dear Tim. It's a vocation—a calling. Not everyone can do this type of job, and we've been gifted with skills that other people probably don't have to fit the bill.'

Tim's face lit up. 'Wow, I never really thought of it like that. You mean—our destiny?'

'That's exactly right.'

'So, you go away and have a jolly good holiday with your parents and the girls. That monster, Lyle, completely ruined Eddie and Meg's lives—with Patty not far behind them—so they need to spend time together and learn how to re-socialise with ordinary people.'

Tim looked down, scuffing the floor with his shoes. 'Don't forget also that I'm still attempting to get over Mary's demise. It'll be a change to be able to mix in a non-threatening way for just a short time—a new beginning for each one of us.'

Ann's face flushed. 'Just make sure you come back—because when you do, there'll be another puzzle waiting for you to unravel.'

****THE END****

Author   Patricia Snelling

Patricia, known as Trish, grew up in a small town in New Zealand. From the age of five, she rode horses which her family owned and trained, often winning prizes in the local horse shows.
Having completed her nursing studies and qualifying as a Registered Nurse, Patricia spent six years abroad, living in Australia, England, and Europe. She returned to Auckland to start a family.
After forty years of nursing, she retired to live on the Hibiscus Coast, where she finds pleasure in being a doting grandmother and writing books. Patricia first started out writing novels in the Romantic Suspense genre and now produces Cosy Crime Mysteries. She has a yen for stories about social justice, particularly involving whistleblowers. All of her novels are set in New Zealand.

VISIT ME:

patriciasnelling.com

https://www.facebook.com/PatriciaSnellingAuthor/

https://www.instagram.com/patriciasnellingnovels/

I would love to receive an honest review if you wish to leave one on any online website or your own blog. Thank you!